Dining With
the Dictator

# Dining With
# the Dictator

# DANY
# LAFERRIÈRE

Translated by David Homel

Coach House Press
Toronto

Copyright © 1994 Coach House Press
*First published as Le goût des jeunes filles by VLB Editeur in 1992*
Copyright © 1992 VLB Editeur
English Translation Copyright © 1994 David Homel

Published with the assistance of the Canada Council, the
Department of Canadian Heritage, the Ontario Arts
Council, and the Ontario Publishing Centre.

Coach House Press
50 Prince Arthur Avenue, Suite 107
Toronto, Canada M5R 1B5

FIRST EDITION
Printed in Canada

Canadian Cataloguing in Publication Data
Laferrière, Dany
[*Goût des jeunes filles.* English]
*Dining with the dictator*
Translation of: *Le goût des jeunes filles.*
ISBN 0-88910-480-8

I. Title. II. Title: *Goût des jeunes filles.* English.

PS8573. A44G613 1994   C843'.54   C94-931743-8
PR9199.3.L34G613 1994

"For my shipwrecked beauty
The street-urchin's music!"

—Magloire Saint-Aude

For the men in my family:

For my grandfather, who loved his roses.

For my father, forever absent, who died in
New York from thirty years of exile.

For my uncle Yves, forever present, whom
I undertook to forget.

For Christophe Charles, the husband of
my only sister, who wrote a book on
Magloire Saint-Aude.

For all these men—sincere, courageous
and honest, each in his own way—who, I
hope, one day, will find someone to give
them voice.

Excuse me for saying it here, but only
women have counted for me.

—D. L.

# Twenty Years Later, in a Little House in Miami

I went down to Little Haiti to pick up a package at my aunts' house. Two of my aunts live in Miami (Aunt Raymonde and Aunt Ninine). The rest of the family is still in Port-au-Prince. My aunts live near North Miami Avenue, ten minutes' walk from Notre Dame church. Aunt Ninine works in a little souvenir stand at the airport, while Aunt Raymonde spends her nights in the terminal ward at Jackson Hospital. Aunt Ninine hadn't come back from the airport yet, and already Aunt Raymonde was on her way out to work. She gave me the package my mother sent me. My mother has my address in Miami, but everything she sends me has to pass through her sisters. That way, she's sure I'll keep in touch with them. Once a week, Wednesday or Friday, I stop by to see them. No normal human being can face Aunt Raymonde more than once a week.

"I'm not going to work just yet," she told me, tidying up her tiny room that was full to the ceiling with the most incredible collection of unlikely objects.

"Aunt Raymonde …"

"I have too much to do." She gave a mighty sigh. "I have to stop by Hall's to make my last payment and pick up a dress. It's yellow dacron, I bought for Renée, she wrote me last month that she didn't have anything to wear to church, though I don't even have the time to go to church, may the Lord forgive me." She crossed herself quickly. "I don't need to ask His forgiveness, He knows, He sees the life I lead here, here in Miami, in the hell that's called Miami."

Shooting broke out on the television. A little black-and-white set balancing atop a mountain of papers and magazines: *The Miami Herald, Ebony, The Amsterdam News, Free Black Press.* Aunt Raymonde lives off coffee and the TV news. She must drink a hundred cups of scalding-hot coffee a day.

"Look what happened this morning," she said, pointing at the television screen. "The woman was at home when two men broke into her kitchen. She didn't even have time to ask them what they wanted—they shot her in the head. Then they poured gasoline on her and set the place on fire. The neighbors called the police. When they brought her into Jackson, she was still alive, if you want to call it that. What was left of her kept quivering and shaking … Three hours she suffered, and I hear they didn't even find anything worth stealing, maybe they didn't break in for that … It's Satan's work, Satan has stolen the soul of this country, O, Babylon, thrice Babylon, when

10

will this ordeal ever end?"

Aunt Raymonde paced through the room in her slip and bra, searching feverishly for a pair of stockings.

"The police caught them in a house in Miami Beach. I heard they were Cubans who just arrived last week. What do you expect? People come to this country and a week later they're dumped in the street like a pack of old rags. Did you hear about ...?"

She stopped to slip on her white nurse's stockings. Her shoes awaited her by the bedside table.

"... The man from Maryland, a family man, they say he lost his job. He went home—oh, hell, I left the iron on the board!"

Aunt Raymonde rushed to the ironing board and grabbed the iron just in time.

"What was I saying? Oh, yes, the man kissed his wife and kids the way he did every day, he took a shower, he changed his clothes, he ate his supper and went to bed ..."

"Did they report whether he made love to his wife?" I asked innocently.

"They didn't talk about that," Aunt Raymonde replied, before realizing she'd walked into a trap. "Why do you always ask things like that, you little whippersnapper?" A smile pulled at her lips. "Let me finish. The next day, he left his house like he was going to work, right on time. Instead, he went to the bank and drew out enough money to buy a gun. Then he went to a McDonald's and started shooting."

There was a long pause.

"That's America, son."

She finished ironing her white dress. We went into

11

the next room. Aunt Raymonde put on an old gray frock.

"Look at these dirty dishes. If I don't wash them they'll stay here till the end of time. I have to do everything in this house. I work twelve hours a day at Jackson and make just enough money to eat and buy a new dress once in a while—when you work at a hospital, you always have to be impeccably dressed." She lifted her head proudly. "If there's any left over, I send it to Port-au-Prince. The rest goes to paying the bills. Look at this." She shook a bundle of tightly bound brown envelopes. "I sell my blood to the white man to pay these things, and remember, I never spend a penny foolishly ... Just the bare essentials. I can't live without eating or drinking, or without electricity, I have to listen to the news on TV, and there's the newspapers, too, luckily they don't cost me anything because I get them at the hospital. We get every newspaper in the country, well, almost every one, and I read them all, I never miss a single one ..."

"Then you bring them back here."

She turned and stared at me, as if she'd forgotten I was there.

"Only when there's an article that really interests me," she said sharply, glancing at the pile of papers underneath the TV set. "At the hospital, the only thing people care about are soap operas. I don't know how they get along, but I'm the kind of person who needs to know what's happening in Russia, and Germany, and South Africa ... I have a patient, she's got cancer all over her body, she's always telling me, 'Ray,' she calls me Ray, 'I don't see what listening to the news the way you do is going to do for you, except give you an ulcer.' She's right. Yesterday, for instance, I got back here, exhausted, I lay down, turned on the TV, and bang! pictures of Haitian refugees. The owner of the boat took their money and promised to bring them here, but when the American Coast Guard showed up, he dropped them in the middle of the ocean and disappeared."

"How could he disappear if the boat was in the middle of the ocean? Did he swim back to Haiti or go up in smoke?"

Aunt Raymonde waved off my question as if it were meaningless.

"When they were finally rescued, the people were half-dead of thirst. Which is why I haven't eaten anything since last night. I can't eat when others are hungry ... Can you tell me why they only have that kind of news on TV?"

She looked me straight in the eye. Did she really expect an answer? I doubted it. Aunt Raymonde never accepts anything from anyone. She likes to complain, but don't try and console her.

"All I do is work. I work, I come home, I have something to eat, even if I don't have an appetite, the food stays right here, half way down, but I try to eat anyway, then I take a laxative and lie down, no, I can't lie down, I don't have the time, I have to do everything in this house. There's no man here, I'm alone with Ninine and I have to take care of everything. I ordered a refrigerator the day before yesterday because the other one was too old. It stopped making ice, even if it was a Westinghouse, which is a good brand, but what do you expect, everything comes to an end ... My end is in sight, too, I'm going to die, I feel weary, my arms have no more strength, what do you expect, they've worked too much, I work like a horse ...

13

My legs won't carry me any more. What did I do to deserve this fate? I never killed anyone. I spent my whole life doing good. Everything I have, I give away. Now I have nothing but this poor body ... Sometimes I wish I could trade this old Raymonde in for a new one."

She burst out laughing. An innocent, almost childlike laugh.

"What was I saying? Oh, yes, the man came and dumped the fridge right in front of the house, even though I'd made it clear I wanted him to go through the yard, I left the gate open on purpose for him, but he couldn't care less. I paid him first, and you should never do that. That was a terrible mistake."

"Did you carry the refrigerator inside?"

"I tried." She smiled slyly. "But when the fellows who work in the garage across the street saw me, they came running out to help. Why? Because I know how to act with people, I talk to everyone, I'm no snob, that's what I always tell Ninine, but Ninine has always been that way, she chooses the people she wishes to speak to, but I'm a democrat, like your father, I know everyone's business and everyone knows my life. My life is an open book. There are no secrets." She looked me in the eye. "Yesterday, for instance, I sent money to Gilberte because she's having problems, and when she has problems, guess who she calls on? Mind you, I have nothing against helping her, I don't want her to go begging from a man, that would be unacceptable, no daughter of Da ever humiliated herself that way. The result? There's no man in this family—true, there was one, that was your father, and he wasn't just any man ... Men? We don't need them. What good are they,

14

anyway? What would I do with a man? What I really need is a millionaire, no, a billionaire, these days a million doesn't go far, he'd have to be half-dead, too, with two or three years to live, but no more, it gets wearisome in the end, everything that lasts too long wears out its welcome."

She finished dressing. I picked up the package from the table in the dining room. She gave me a military salute.

"All ready for battle. My job's worse than the army. I'm on call twenty-four hours a day, day and night, sometimes I go three days straight. Of course, they do pay me." Her voice wavered. Suddenly she was on the brink of tears. "But I'm not young any more, I don't have the strength for it ..."

She came closer to me and looked me in the eye. I lowered my gaze.

"Look at me."

She stuck her finger in my face.

"You're quiet all of a sudden! You're waiting for me to die."

I kept my head down. Her eyes burned. Her bony hand jerked my chin up.

"How can you say such a thing, Aunt Raymonde?"

Her finger was sharper than a switchblade.

"Your book is a lie from the first page to the last."

I should have known. Everything else was just a warm-up. The real point was The Book. A few months ago, I published a little book about my childhood and gave her a copy. She told me she'd read it right away, in three days time. Part of it at home, part at the hospital. Strange, but she never mentioned the book again. I tried once or twice to coax something out of her. Nothing. Now, today, it all comes out.

"Nothing is true in that book."

"Nothing?"

"Nothing," she said, challenging me.

Aunt Raymonde strode over to the little shelf where my book sat, next to some recipe collections. She picked it up, opened it, sniffed at it as if it gave off a bad odor. I decided to avoid confrontation.

"Of course, Aunt Raymonde. It's fiction."

Naturally, she wasn't swayed by that argument.

"Oh, no, you're not going to get away that easy. When it's just fiction, you don't put people's names in it."

"Actually, it's a mixture of fiction and reality."

"You don't need to tell me what it is! I can still read, by the grace of God."

She paged quickly through the book.

"Where did you get that story about Timise?"

"Actually, it happened to Oginé, but for my book, it was better with Timise."

"Very nice!" She smiled contemptuously. "What if Timise reads your book?"

"Aunt Raymonde, Timise doesn't know how to read."

She burst out laughing. The telephone rang. She ran to pick it up. There was a brief conversation.

"That was the hospital … It's always the hospital, and it'll always be the hospital. Who else would ever think of calling Raymonde? The only man who remembered my birthday is dead, and that was my father."

Dangerous territory. Very dangerous. I kept quiet, hoping that her monologue would take another tack.

16

"Everything you wrote about my father was lies."

Apparently, I wasn't going to be spared. Even if I did draw a very fair portrait of my grandfather.

"He was my grandfather, Aunt Raymonde," I stammered.

"I know. But that doesn't mean you knew him."

"A grandfather is different from a father. I mean, he might be the same person, but he has two different functions."

She stared at me a moment or two, speechless, as if she had missed something.

"Why didn't you talk about our family's solidarity?"

"I did talk about my grandmother."

I was ashamed when I said it. Aunt Raymonde smiled. Radiantly. How beautiful she must have been!

"That part was fine. You always loved your grandmother."

We sat in silence for a moment. Da (my grandmother) was among us. A brief truce.

"Why didn't you describe how my father sacrificed for our education? Back in those days, girls were sent to learn sewing at Madame Julie's, but my father—"

"Yes, of course, Aunt Raymonde, but—"

"Let me finish, young man. You had your opportunity, and now everyone knows everything about us, people I don't know and I'll never know … My father sent us to Port-au-Prince to study. You can't imagine what that meant back then. This man," she said, pointing to the large photograph of my grandfather that hung above the telephone, "this man sacrificed himself for his daughters, and that's not in your novel."

17

She brought her hand down hard on the book. Funny, but I felt as though I'd been slapped. Even if Aunt Raymonde had told me another version ten years ago, completely different from this one. Somehow I didn't think it was the right time to point that out.

"Da's daughters always faced adversity together. We always stuck together and we're going to stay that way. No man can separate us. There was only one man in this family and he was your father, he was the only one ... I know that Gilberte had lovers, and Ninine, too, from time to time, but it was always a passing fancy, it never counted for very much."

I wanted to tell her it was her fault that everything turned out this way, that she'd poisoned her sisters' lives with her obsession with one man. But what good would that have done?

"I had my offers, too," she said with a challenge in her voice, "but I chose my family, and as long as my sisters need me, I'll be there. A good captain never abandons ship in a storm."

"What storm, Aunt Raymonde?"

"The storm of life, young man."

She snapped up the pile of bills and slipped them into her right front pocket. She picked up a scarf on the way out—she had a slight cold—and crossed the living-room without a glance into the big oval mirror. Before I knew it, Aunt Raymonde was out in the street. I ran to get my car and caught up to her at the corner.

"Aunt Raymonde, I can drop you off."

"No, thank you."

"I've got plenty of time."

18

"The bus goes right by the hospital."

"It's no trouble … Just a few blocks out of my way."

"You won't have to go out of your way."

I didn't know what to do.

"Really, it's on the way, Aunt Raymonde, I *want* to drive you to work, it would be a pleasure."

"Don't bother. Here comes my bus."

I watched her climb on board. She grasped her bag tightly under her right arm. She didn't look back. She wasn't angry with me—she was furious. Furious at life.

Just before it was too late, she turned around. Her eyes piercing. A slight smile on her lips.

"In any case," she called, "you got enough material today to keep you writing for a week."

"What are you talking about?" I called back as the bus pulled away.

She tapped her index finger against her temple as if to remind me that she was no fool.

# The Bathroom Is My Sanctuary

## 1

I love reading my mail in the bathtub. With the water not too hot. Thinking about nothing. The package on the floor, just below my left hand. My ration of letters (one from Aunt Gilberte, another from Aunt Renée and two from my mother). My mother prefers to send me two short letters instead of one long one. The first is more technical, full of practical advice: about vegetables, and how sleep heals the body, how carrots are good for your eyes, the dangers of venereal disease and girls who are out to get pregnant without your consent and who will take you to court where you'll spend years of your life, the advantages of taking a hot bath before bed, about two-faced and jealous friends, cod-liver oil, food poisoning, the need to get a haircut every two weeks and, most of all, how I should never forget that she, my mother, is the only person in the

20

world in whom I can have absolute trust. The second letter is more mystical. My mother tells me about Jesus, who should be my partner in everything I do. No one can succeed without Him. He's a brother, a friend, a companion, a faithful associate. He asks nothing for his troubles, not even a penny; He just wants to know what I'm doing. "His advice is always fair," my mother writes. "Put your life in His hands." My mother talks about Jesus as if she knew Him personally. I'm sure she does. I believe in her faith. My mother's letters used to bring a smile to my face. Now, more and more, I believe that this inoffensive, fragile, humble, modest woman somehow holds the world's destiny in her hands. The world will continue to exist as long as she's among the living. I feel her presence in this room. I press my feet against my backside in the fetal position. My painful birth. A few days later, my mother's breast! Those were good days! The sweetness of mother's milk— unfortunately, not sweet enough for my taste. If I'd had a say, it would have contained more sugar. I put my head under water. Water, marvelous water. In the great debate between fire and water that's been raging since the beginning of time, I've always been on the side of water. I'm an aquatic animal. I float, motionless. The dead man's float. The drowned man. One of the elements of water. Never to thirst again. I doze off for a few seconds. The water's slow world. The cyclical life. I wake up gradually. So much happiness is frightening. I was slipping peacefully into another universe. I dry my hands and pick up the letters all wrapped in pages of *Le Nouvelliste*. I carefully untie the package, making sure not to tear the thin newsprint. I read the newspaper that's crumpled and torn in places, and discover that one of my old friends has become a minister in the government, while the other is wanted by the police. The usual moment of reflection. I assimilate the news, then the painful questioning begins. What have I become? Why aren't I back there? Can I change my life? Usually, these questions steal five minutes of my time. Then I touch the object. A book. My mother always sends me my friends' books. Impatiently, I tear away the last sheet of paper. A book by Magloire Saint-Aude. The old copy from when I was a teenager. I reread my mother's letter. Between two pieces of advice (I must have skipped a few paragraphs the first time), she tells how she found the book in her chest of drawers. She came upon it by accident, and now she's sending it to me, she tells me in her simple manner. Then she adds that Miki ("You remember her, dear, she lived just across the street") has a shop that sells jewelry and fabric, and that she goes to Miami on a regular basis to pick up stock. She gave her my telephone number.

I couldn't take my eyes off the battered cover of Magloire Saint-Aude's book of poems.

## 2

The telephone rings. It's Miki. I know it is. Destiny, said Borges—or was it some Arab poet?—is a blind camel. It can pass over the same spot three times and never know it. It happens all the time. You forget that someone even exists, then one day, you hear their name a half-dozen times. Why? I have no idea. Right now, I'm trying to get out of the bathtub without getting my letters wet, without dropping

22

the book in the water, or flooding the floor and, if I can, before Miki hangs up. There, I did it. Good work. I pick up the receiver. Of course it's Miki. We all have days like that.

"Is that you?"

"It's me. How are you, Miki?"

No answer.

"Your voice has changed. It's gotten deeper."

"I'm almost forty, Miki."

"Don't talk about getting old ... How are you doing?"

"You first."

"Okay. What about you?" she insisted.

"Okay."

"What are you up to? Oh, I know," Miki said quickly, "Marie-Michèle saw your picture in an American magazine. You're getting famous."

"What about you?"

"Oh, nothing ... Didn't your mother tell you?"

"She said you have a shop. I'm happy for you. How's it going?"

"I can't complain ... Did you hear about what happened to Choupette?"

Her voice turned serious.

"No," I shouted into the phone. "No bad news!"

"You're the boss," Miki said calmly. "Still, you should know. It was in the papers."

"Okay, go ahead and tell me."

"You know that Choupette and Papa were living together for a while. He left his wife and family for her."

"Excuse me, Miki, but I haven't heard a word about Choupette since that famous weekend."

"Of course," said Miki. "Well, they were together. I

saw less and less of Choupette. Papa used to fly into these crazy fits of jealousy, so I heard, but Choupette couldn't have cared less. She lived like she'd always lived. She went crazy over some guitar player. Papa walked in on them in a hotel room in Delmas. I'm sure someone told Papa they'd be there. Anyway, Choupette never was very discreet, as you know … According to *Le Nouvelliste,* Papa put three bullets into the guy. Luckily, he didn't hit any vital organs, but the guy's been in a wheelchair ever since … I saw Choupette two days after the shooting, and she looked pretty shook up. I'll never forget her tone of voice when she talked about Papa. 'How could I have known he loved me, since no one's ever loved me?' I never saw them again … That's all. Sorry for taking up your time."

"No, I'm glad you told me."

There was a pause.

"I have to go now," Miki said. "I have someone on the other line."

Another pause.

"Bye, Miki."

"Bye, yourself. I'll call you again, and we'll get together for a drink sometime."

"Good idea."

Twenty years from now will be soon enough. I'll be fifty-nine. Saint-Aude's age when he died.


# 3


I went back to the bathroom and slipped into the warm water that protects me from time and all the world's misfortunes. I opened Saint-Aude's book and read the poet's last lines:

> This, the last romance
> Love that is pale and solemn ...
>
> These, the last fires
>
> These, the last games
>
> Of the hollow clown
> Of my staring demise
> Here on the quays of silence.

Saint-Aude never wrote another line in his life.

## 4

Still in the bath. This time, with the phone close at hand. I thought of Miki. Even the telephone couldn't distort her wonderful voice. It brought to mind the weekend I spent in her house, some twenty-five years ago. The weekend that changed everything.

## 5

Three hours later, I was engaged in conversation in front of the little oval mirror. Myself and the Other.

OTHER  Aren't you forgetting that Magloire Saint-

Aude never had to worry while Duvalier was in power?

SELF  Isn't that for the best?

OTHER  Maybe, but do you want to know why he was so free?

SELF  If you want to tell me.

OTHER  See? You're denying it already.

SELF  I'd rather have Saint-Aude free on the streets of Port-au-Prince than rotting away in Duvalier's prisons.

OTHER  He was Duvalier's friend till the end. They even died the same year.

SELF  So what? Saint-Aude was never a political poet.

OTHER  Yet he was at the origins of the Duvalier ideology.

SELF  Prove it.

OTHER  In June of 1938, your Saint-Aude signed *Le manifeste des griots,* the Caribbean equivalent of Hitler's *Mein Kampf.* Who signed with him? Carl Brouard, another anarchist poet who enjoyed a state funeral when he died, the shadowy Lorimer Denis and the sinister Duvalier himself.

SELF  You're going a little too far. You know the manifesto created increased awareness of nationhood.

OTHER  Awareness of Duvalierism, that is. Even during the darkest years of the dictatorship, Saint-Aude never repudiated Duvalier.

SELF  But his work did.

OTHER  Explain yourself.

SELF  Saint-Aude's work is the negation of his political thought.

OTHER  Which proves he's a fake.

SELF  You're not convincing me, brother …

Silence fell upon us. We evaluated each other like boxers at the weigh-in.

OTHER  So, for you, is he still the greatest poet of the Americas?

SELF  I'm afraid so!

# 6

The phone rang again. This time it was within reach. I wouldn't have to get the bathmat wet.

"It's me again, Miki."

"Yes?"

"I forgot to tell you something."

"I'm listening."

"Don't worry. It's good news. Look on page sixty-three of *Vogue* this month. Do you remember Marie-Michèle?"

"Yes. Now what?"

"It's a surprise. Bye, *ciao* ..."

"*Ciao*, Miki."

# 7

I'll buy *Vogue* later. Right now, nothing will make me leave this bathtub. I turn on the hot water. I soap myself up again. Black skin, white mask. I continue my reading of Saint-Aude. Twenty-five years ago, I hadn't noticed the afterword on the last page of the book.

I knew nothing about André Breton at the time. His

influential article came out in the fall of 1945. Right after the war.

Breton's comments opened the doors for Saint-Aude. It's true that Saint-Aude closed them all, one after the other. He didn't need Breton to guide him through the gates of hell. He would see to his own fall, all by himself. And with such care!

> Twelve or fifteen lines, no more, I understand your desire: the philosopher's stone, or almost, the unheard note that tames the tumult, the single gear that puts the wheel of destiny on the road to ecstasy. We may wonder who, since the Sphinx, has, within such limits, succeeded in halting the wanderer. In French poetry, there has been Scève, Nerval, Mallarmé, Apollinaire … You know that everything is too undisciplined today. One exception springs to mind: Magloire Saint-Aude.
> —André Breton

Later, in 1953, Jean Brierre met the poet and returned with this definitive portrait.

> This square-faced coolie, wearing a half-smile implicit in his words, lives a nocturnal existence, in lamplight, reflection, shadow. His Oriental eyes that burn with quiet malice are perfect

28

companions for the two graven lines
that set off his lips and the vestigial
laughter that rolls low in his throat like
an affected cough.

I try and see how long I can stay under water without breathing. A little over a minute. More than six minutes, and another universe will welcome me. A practitioner of voodoo can spend more than three days under water. Saint-Aude lived on the borders of that world.

## 8

Two women were ahead of me in the line. One black, one white. Both enormous. Democracy, American style. Their carts overflowing with the fruits of the earth. Canned food, industrial-quantity meat, piles of spaghetti, bottles of Coke, eggs, rice, milk, bananas, etc. I picked up *Vogue* and opened it right to the photo of Marie-Michèle. A full page.

## 9

On the way back, I kept Marie-Michèle's picture on the seat next to me. I listened to Skah Shah's latest hit. Not bad. I got on the expressway instead of going home. The last place in America where you can dream. I passed the exit to Little Haiti and took U.S. 1 toward Key West. To the end of America. Mile zero. I checked into the southernmost

29

motel. A room with a view of the Atlantic. I closed the curtains. Nothing to see out there. I've always preferred a good bathroom to any ocean. I ran the bath, then slipped gently into the tub. I like the close quarters of the tub. The fetal position it imposes. No one knows where I am. I am in America; that's enough. My life has become so simple it involves but a single person. Me. Suddenly I got the urge to make a little, low-budget film, without professional actors, and the smallest possible crew. A three-day shoot. Hand-held camera. Very home-movie. Black and white, of course. Just for myself. No one else would see it. I would screen it privately for an audience of one in my bathtub.

On a rainy day, of course.


# 10

Quiet on the set!

# Weekend in Port-au-Prince

*A Film Written, Directed and Produced*
*by Dany Laferrière*

## CREDITS

| | |
|---|---|
| *The Girls* | Choupette |
| | Pasqualine |
| | Marie-Flore |
| | Marie-Erna |
| | Marie-Michèle |
| | Michaëlle (Miki) |
| | |
| *The Women* | Marie (my mother) |
| | Aunt Raymonde |
| | Aunt Ninine |
| | Aunt Gilberte |
| | Aunt Renée |
| | |
| *The Men* | Papa |
| | Frank |
| | |
| *The Boys* | Gégé |
| | Dany |

| *Music* | Tabou Combo |
| | Les Shleu Shleu |
| | Bossa Combo |
| | Shupa Shupa |
| | Les Gypsies |
| | Les Difficiles (from Pétionville) |

*Weather*

Ninety degrees in the shade. Humid. Rain
expected by the end of the weekend.

| *Settings* | Olympia Cinema |
| | Macaya Bar |
| | Doc's Place |
| | The Portail Léogâne |
| | Place Sainte-Anne |
| | Fort Dimanche |
| | Anson Music Center |
| | National Bar |
| | Pasqualine's place (in Pétionville) |
| | Miki's place |
| | My mother and my aunts' house |

| | |
|---|---|
| *Walk-Ons* | Doc |
| | The policeman from the Portail |
| |     Léogâne station |
| | The Macaya Bar whore |
| | The shark |
| | The guitar player |
| | The singer |
| | The *Vogue* photographer |
| | The *Rolling Stone* journalist |
| | The taxi driver |
| | The pimp |
| | Sylvana, the prostitute from Le Cap |
| | The scalpers |

The action takes place in Port-au-Prince at the end of April, 1971. The 1960s have just come to Haiti. Ten years late. As usual.

## Voice Over

I look out the window of my room. A light rain is falling. Cars pass with whispering tires. Miki's house is on the other side of the street. Full of laughter and shouting and girls. Miki lives alone, but she has plenty of friends. Every day, there are always two or three cars parked in front of her door, ready to head for the beach, a restaurant in the hills or a dance. Meanwhile, I study my algebra. And it's not just Miki. Here comes Pasqualine, stretching like a Persian cat. Marie-Michèle is a bit of a snob, and Choupette is as foul-mouthed as a fishmonger. Marie-Erna's haughty pout and Marie-Flore's firm backside. The men keep changing. I take up position by the window in my room upstairs. I dream of the day when I, too, will go to heaven, across the street. To get there, they say, you have to die first. I'm willing to risk it.

## SCENE I

# Friday Afternoon

On the horizon of fever
—M. S.-A.

Choupette poured ketchup and salt and pepper on her chicken basket, then sprinkled vinegar over the whole thing. Marie-Flore went on examining the menu. Waiter number seven lost patience and ran back to pick up the order on the kitchen counter. Marie-Flore and Miki headed for the ladies' room. Marie-Erna caught number seven on the fly and asked for fish and a salad. Pasqualine finished her rum on the rocks and ordered strawberry ice cream. The sun poured into the National Bar. The window glass was burning hot. More girls arrived and went to the back.

The old 1957 Buick pointed its rear end toward the Oso Blanco butcher shop, then glided into the National Bar's parking lot.

"Look who's coming," said Pasqualine.

"It's Papa," Marie-Erna called. "Let's act like we don't recognize him."

"You know him, do you?" Choupette asked with a serious look.

The girls started laughing for no good reason. Suddenly, Marie-Erna's laughter turned to sobs.

"What's the matter with you?" Marie-Michèle asked her.

She went on sobbing, twice as hard.

"What's the matter, or don't you know?" Marie-Michèle insisted.

"Nothing," Marie-Erna finally managed to say.

"Nothing!" Pasqualine cried.

Choupette gave Marie-Erna a kleenex, and she blew her nose noisily.

"What's the matter with you?" Marie-Michèle repeated.

"Nothing's the matter with her," Choupette said. "That's not the first time she's pulled that stunt on me."

"It's her nerves, maybe," Pasqualine suggested.

"I heard that's the way epileptics act," Marie-Michèle said.

"I'm not an epileptic. I've always been that way. When I laugh too hard, when it's too beautiful a day, I start to cry."

"I've never seen anything like it," Pasqualine laughed. "You must be allergic to happiness."

"I guess that's it." Marie-Erna smiled sadly.

"Does it happen when you fuck?" Choupette joked.

"I won!" shouted Pasqualine, who had been busy eating her strawberry ice cream. "I bet Miki a scarf that you

38

couldn't go ten minutes without talking about sex, and it's been exactly six minutes and thirty-eight seconds."

"What you really mean," Choupette answered with a smile, "is that I went more than six minutes without talking about sex!"

Everyone broke up.

"Shit, Choupette, you do it on purpose," cried Marie-Erna, then she dissolved into sobs.

"Did someone see where Papa went?" asked Marie-Michèle.

"Here he comes," said Pasqualine.

Papa went into the food store to buy a flint for his lighter. The guy at the cash, the one with the pimply red nose, told him to try down at the Petite Europe. Papa crossed the street, glanced quickly at the Buick sparkling in the sun, then pushed open the National Bar's glass door. Just then, number nine lowered the two blinds to get the right mixture of light and shadow in the tiny, well-lit room with a half-dozen tables.

The group changed tables and sat in the sun. Marie-Flore and Miki came out of the ladies' room, each wearing a hibiscus behind her ear. Their hair, streaming with licorice water, was combed in the flapper style, with a part down the middle. Marie-Flore emptied her glass of orangeade in one gulp and went fishing for the cherry at the bottom with a long, plastic swizzle-stick. Marie-Erna half-read the directions on the bottle of pomade that sat on the table, then slipped the container into her bag.

To keep your hair looking shiny and
young, take a bit of beef marrow in your

hands, then massage your scalp lightly
until your hair is covered to the ends.


Miki shook her head and tiny drops of water flew
every which way.

"You owe me a scarf," Pasqualine told her.

Miki shot Choupette a quick look.

"At least I went more than five minutes," Choupette
said softly in her own defence.

Papa sat at a table that gave him a good view of his
Buick. The black mass of the old Buick spread like a pud-
dle of India ink. Papa pretended to study the menu, but he
kept glancing over at the girls.

"What's eating him?" Miki asked in a low voice.

"Choupette put him in quarantine," Marie-Erna told
her.

"What did he do to you?" Miki asked worriedly.

"Nothing," said Choupette. "I just got tired of having
him on me all the time."

"*Around* me," Marie-Michèle corrected her. "*Around*
me, not *on* me, Choupette."

"Don't you think I know?"

"Shit, Choupette," Miki protested, "don't you ever
stop thinking about it, for just one minute?"

"Sure," said Choupette. "When I'm doing it."

Marie-Flore jumped up and changed places with
Marie-Erna to be closer to Papa.

"I can't stand to see him eat all by himself," Marie-
Flore said.

Miki changed places with Pasqualine and ended up
next to Marie-Erna. Marie-Flore searched for a cigarette in

40

her bag, found one and put it to her lips with infinite slowness until Papa got the hint and lit it for her. Choupette fidgeted on her chair and looked at her watch. Number seven picked up the empty glasses, wiped the table top and put down a clean ashtray.

"Why do you keep looking at your watch?" Miki asked.

"I wish time would stop."

"Do you have something better to do?" Miki wondered.

"No, nothing," said Choupette, shrugging her shoulders. "I don't like to waste time, that's all."

"But if you have nothing else to do ..."

"That's the point," Choupette told her. "Time is most precious when you have nothing to do."

"That's a good one," Marie-Erna put in. "Where the hell did you find that?"

"Up your ass."

"Go fuck yourself!" Marie-Erna shouted.

"You're not going to start all over again!" Miki shouted. "Anyway, who cares, I'm getting out of here."

The girls jumped up and ran for the door. Waiter number seven flew into a panic. Number nine tried to catch them. Papa motioned to number seven to put it on his tab. Peace returned to the bar.

Papa opened the car door and the girls got in. Everyone but Choupette.

"Sit next to me," Miki told her.

"I'd rather take a taxi."

"Why?" Pasqualine asked her.

"Because," Choupette snapped.

Miki and Pasqualine got out and pushed Choupette

into the car.

"Whatever goes on between a man and a woman is none of my business," Marie-Erna stated.

"What did you do to her?" Marie-Michèle asked Papa.

"I didn't do anything," he said plaintively.

"That's the problem," Choupette shot back. "I'm young, I want something to happen. I want something terrible to happen to me … Instead, I end up with this old wreck."

"You're exaggerating, Choupette," Marie-Erna snapped.

"You can have him if you want him," Choupette hissed.

"I never touch what doesn't belong to me," Marie-Erna answered.

"Get off it!" Choupette barked. "That's all that bitch ever does."

"You're a lucky man, Papa," Marie-Michèle said with a half-smile. "You've got women fighting over you."

"I didn't do anything," Papa said as he drove toward the center of town.

"You can shut up now," Choupette told him. "Everyone knows you never do anything."

"Where are we going?" Marie-Michèle asked.

"Does it matter?" Miki said.

"It does when I'm in this car," Marie-Michèle replied.

"We're going nowhere, baby. Everything that's happening is happening in this car."

Pasqualine let loose a terrible high-pitched scream. Marie-Flore's breasts did a dance. The afternoon held on for dear life.

# A Boy with a Pointy Chin, Slant-Eyes and No Forehead

Longer than my shadow
—M. S.-A.

Gégé came by the house. I was pretending to study. I had a physics test the next Monday. Aunt Renée was standing in front of me, peeling an orange, and the smell made me queasy. I have respiratory troubles, and I've always been sensitive to smells. Aunt Ninine was trying on a yellow dress stuck full of pins in front of the oval mirror. I waited till she turned her back on me, then I slipped out to meet Gégé. My mother won't let me hang out with him. Aunt Gilberte says that Gégé looks like the devil himself.

Gégé never has had any luck with girls. He has a pointy chin, slanted eyes and no forehead. They call him the Mongol. There was a guy from the Pétion *lycée*, and Gégé put out his eye. The eye was all slimy, and it rolled along the ground. Gégé put his right foot on it and popped it. My mother is afraid of what I might do when I'm with Gégé. My mother doesn't know how right she is. I admit it, I follow him around like a puppy. It's one way of getting out from under my mother's and my aunts' skirts. Those women treat me like a child! Besides, with Gégé, I'm never bored. Here, there's nothing to do. I study my lessons and do my homework (I'm a good student); otherwise, I sit on the front steps and watch the people go by. That's it. That's all I do in the afternoon. Sometimes, I watch the clouds go by. I spend hours watching the clouds. The clouds traveling. I wonder what I could have done with all the time I wasted watching the clouds. The clouds, or the moon. The moon takes even more time.

When I met Gégé, everything changed. At first, I thought he was willing to be my friend just to copy my homework. Then I realized that school meant nothing to Gégé. Every day, he invented a game more dangerous than the one the day before. He taught me the train game. We would lie down on the rails and wait for the train. When it came you had to wait to the last second before getting out of the way. Obviously, I was always the first to get up. Finally, we dropped that game (whew!) for one even more dangerous (oh, no!). One day, I went with him to school, the day before the algebra test. We went into the court-yard. There wasn't a soul around. It was already dark. We were walking on our tiptoes, keeping close to the wall, when I felt something cold, there, between my legs. At first, I didn't turn around. I touched Gégé's shoulder. He smiled, that bastard. He'd planned the whole thing. I didn't dare move. Gégé had a little bag, and he took a

44

meatball out of it. The meatball was full of slivers of broken glass, and he threw it to the dog. The dog watched the meatball roll along the ground, a few meters away. He hesitated a second or two, then threw himself on it.

"That'll keep him busy," Gégé said.

"If he eats it, he'll die."

"Maybe you'd rather have him rip your nuts off?"

"No. But killing an animal that way ..."

"He shouldn't eat it then."

"But you know he will."

"Then that'll be his choice."

It looked as though the dog was enjoying the meatball. We went on our way. It was dark inside the school. We headed for the principal's office. Gégé took out a key ring. Once we got there, he went straight to the metal filing cabinets. Five minutes later, he had his hands on the algebra test. Algebra is no problem for me. I could have solved those problems with my eyes closed. Gégé took his time and copied out all the equations, then we left. As we were about to scale the wall, I saw the dog near his doghouse, lying on his back, his eyes wide open. Magnificent black eyes, shining bright. His stomach was quivering ever so slightly. You can see a lot of things in a couple of seconds. Death, for one.

Gégé didn't even bother showing up the next day for the algebra test.

# The City Built on Fifteen Hills

No nation, no master
—M. S.-A.

The 1957 Buick took the corner by the Firestone shop and went down the rue Pavée. Choupette turned on the radio. Marie-Erna laughed with two guys who were driving by in a yellow Subaru.

"You know who that was?" Marie-Erna asked Miki.

"I didn't see."

"Cubano. He was with the singer from Tabou."

"Why didn't you say anything?" Choupette shouted at her.

"I barely had time to wave," Marie-Erna said.

"You know, you're a real bitch," Choupette told her.

"Shit, Choupette, it's not my fault. If the guy wanted to talk to you, he would have stopped."

46

"Who?" asked Marie-Flore, completely out of the picture.

"Cubano," Miki answered.

"Him again," Marie-Flore concluded.

The old 1957 Buick plowed into the afternoon. Colors, people, houses paraded by. A young boy with shining skin bombarded his little sister with water as she ran off. A woman grabbed a man by the collar and bawled him out. A taxi in the middle of the street, out of gas. The hot afternoon breeze. Beads of sweat bloomed and ran down Pasqualine's spine. The Buick stopped of its own accord at the corner where the Shell station is. Papa threw a bucket of water on the Buick's grille that glowed red with thirst, then he hosed down the wheels. Miki ran across the street to buy some sodas. Pasqualine couldn't take it any more; she got out of the Buick and leaned against the door. Marie-Flore headed for a tub of clean water and stuck her head in it. The gas-jockey winked at Papa. It was ninety degrees in the shade. Everyone got back in the car. The 1957 Buick started skipping like a young goat. It really had been thirsty. Choupette finished her soda and threw the bottle out the window.

"Are you crazy or something?" Marie-Michèle exclaimed. "You could have hurt somebody."

"I don't give a damn!" Choupette snarled.

"*Gen yon bébé ke mwen renmen, lan Paramount tou le Samedi,*" Marie-Erna sang.

Tabou Combo's hit.

"Shut up!" Choupette snarled again.

"*Mwen renmen l', mwen renmen l', mwen renmen l','*" everyone sang the chorus but Choupette.

47

"Piss on it," Choupette said.

The Buick turned the corner by the Bank of Nova Scotia to avoid the monster traffic jam in the lower town, then stopped in front of the Anson Music Center. The girls jumped out of the car and slammed the doors. Pasqualine's slender body shimmered in a green dress hardly bigger than a handkerchief. High atop her black heels, she crossed the burning pavement. As she pushed through the revolving door, Marie-Flore turned around half-way and gave Papa a man-eating wink. There was an enormous poster of a pair of naked buttocks devouring a giant hamburger dripping with ketchup above an aquarium full of goldfish. Shupa Shupa's latest record playing at full blast. The needle skipped over a speck of dust. A cool chick with a super Afro shook her blue-jeaned butt. The air conditioning was balm for bodies swimming with sweat. The sweet dark feel of a room filled with water. Pasqualine lit herself a cigarette and cooled out. Relax, if you please, baby. At the back of the room, a guy in a tee-shirt exploded to the sounds of the Gypsies. Marie-Flore slipped a mother-of-pearl comb into her bag. Two girls came in and left with three Bossa Combo records. Subtly, Marie-Erna dropped a tiny flask of perfume into her purse. Choupette wanted to play the latest record by Les Difficiles from Pétionville. The girls yelled at her to let Tabou play, and they scattered when Pasqualine took out an old Gary French record.

Silence. Papa, alone in the Buick, put up all the windows. The *tap-taps* went by with a noise like the soft plop of manure. The landscape was smoky, drowned in metallic light. Papa was sweating. He began to feel sick. His eyes dilated. His mouth was dry. A man passed in front of him with a dozen watches around his wrist. He yelled something at Papa and raised his arm. A woman dragged along a little boy in a sailor suit. Cut left to Bazar La Poste: a pop-bottle neck between two fleshy lips and ivory-white teeth, spilling out pinkish liquid. A little girl pressing her face against the Buick's hot window glass. Slow motion: the red throat of a deep-sea fish gobbling up its food in an enormous aquarium. Zoom in on a roaming hand closing over a pair of earrings. Interior. Papa drowning in his sweat and specks of dust sliding lazily down the car windows in the rustling of liquid silk, red spatters and wild garlands of ectoplasm scratching the retina.

The girls came back. The Buick took off.

RED LIGHT. The whole length of the block, between the rue Pavée and the rue des Césars, four lines of cars waited at the intersection, bumper to bumper. Motors rumbled. Music poured out. American Buicks and Chryslers. French Peugeots and Citroëns. Japanese Toyotas and Datsuns.

GREEN LIGHT. Motors revved. Gear levers ground into first. Cars spread out between the stores, the crowds, the brilliant colors of the posters.

In another few minutes, all those staved-in, repainted jalopies would fan out through Port-au-Prince, the city built on fifteen hills (Saint-Martin, Sans Fil, Bel Air, Canapé Vert, Bourdon, Fort National, Saint-Gérard, Turgeau, Pacot, Morne-à-Turf, Poste-Marchand, Nazon, Bois Verna, Bolosse, Nelhio) with its ant-taxis climbing the heaven-seeking streets.

The old Buick slowed in front of the iron market, turned by the old landing field, then headed up toward Pétionville.

49

SCENE IV

# The Terrible
# Three O'Clock Sun

The flight of empty afternoons
—M. S.-A.

A guy stopped Gégé by the Stadium to find out whether
he'd be coming to the game that night.

"Who's playing?" Gégé wanted to know.

"Bacardi and Don Bosco," the guy told him.

Gégé spat on the ground. The guy was trying to sell
Gégé a ticket.

"I wouldn't buy one if it was half price," Gégé said.

"Sometimes you get more than you bargain for," the
guy answered.

"You know where you can put your ticket," Gégé said
in an even voice.

The guy went looking for another sucker. We went
on our way. Another scalper came up.

50

"I've got good tickets for tomorrow."

"Why would I buy tickets today for tomorrow's game?" Gégé asked.

"It's Racing against Black Eagle."

"Great!" I answered.

Gégé gave me a funny look. The guy stepped up to Gégé and took out the tickets.

"You're wasting your time, man," Gégé told him. "I never pay to get into the Stadium."

"What about him?" The guy pointed in my direction.

"He's with me." Gégé was shouting now. "And he doesn't pay either!"

"No problem," the guy said.

He headed toward the Stadium entrance, where a little group of scalpers had gathered. They all wear the same uniform: white tennis shoes, a tee-shirt and a red or white cap that looks as though it's been screwed onto their heads. I wonder why they always have an orange in their mouths.

When the guy left, Gégé spat on the ground again. I've never seen anyone like Gégé. Always in a rage. I wouldn't want to be his enemy. Being his friend is bad enough.

The street that runs by the Stadium is hell when it gets hot. The big cemetery is on your left as you go down toward the sea. There's no shelter from the sun. The terrible three o'clock sun. It feels as though it's going to hang there for all eternity. A woman was washing her clothes in the ravine, near the cemetery, in a trickle of dirty water. Higher up, a man dropped his trousers (his butt was lashed with black scars) and looked around quickly to

51

make sure no one was coming. Human excrement filled the ravine. Most of it was dry and black, like dead wood. It didn't smell any more; it had been washed by the rain and dried by the sun.

We went down to the Olympia moviehouse. A western was playing. In the lobby was a big poster of a man wearing a hat, legs bowed, staring straight ahead. His nervous fingers grazed his revolver. In a few seconds, someone was going to get shot between the eyes. Gégé doesn't pay at the Olympia either. We walked right past the ticket-taker in his little cage. The theater was in total darkness. I couldn't see past my nose.

"Let's sit in front," said Gégé, pushing me from behind.

Gégé thinks that if he sits in front, he'll see the picture before anybody else does. A man was already there. He had a nervous tic. His whole body trembled. I took a closer look. He was holding pistols in both hands and trying to outdraw John Wayne. A shark. I knew him, his name was Touche.

"Let's go," I told Gégé.

"What's the matter?"

"I don't like this movie."

"Me neither," Gégé said.

We went out slowly, yawning and stretching as if we had been in the theater all day. The guy came out of his cage and grabbed Gégé by the left arm.

"Hey, you, I didn't see you come in!"

"Why would you?" Gégé said.

"What are you talking about?"

"You think we'd pay to see your crummy picture?"

52

The guy looked Gégé in the eye. Gégé didn't flinch. It was a duel. The guy lowered his eyes first.

"I don't want to see you around here again," the guy threatened us, then went into his cage.

Gégé eased out of the moviehouse the way John Wayne would have done it, under the burning sun of a little border town.

"We'll come back whenever we want to," Gégé said.

"Yeah, if there's ever a good picture," I added.

"Bunch of little pests," the guy answered.

"Go take it up the ass," Gégé told him.

The guy changed color.

"Why'd you say that to him?"

"I don't like his mug," Gégé replied.

The sun hadn't moved. I like coming out of a movie and seeing the sun. We kept on walking toward the sea, legs apart like the guys from the OK Corral. We didn't even stop to take a piss. God knows I had to go, but have you ever seen John Wayne piss?

## SCENE V

# The Holy Night Gently Lowers
# Its Butt Upon the City

Upon a hair prefaced by my fingers
—M. S.-A.

Pasqualine's nail-hard body on pointe slices through the blinding light in metallic harshness. The plane of her body bent at the middle. The pure line of young thighs.

Marie-Erna paged through a photo-romance on the sofa. Marie-Flore walked barefoot across the cool cement floor.

The window illuminated the room. A beam of light from the red sunset split it into two moist, shadowy zones.

Miki brushed Pasqualine's silky hair in front of a large oval mirror. Choupette ran out to the Chinaman's and came back with chicken-fried rice on paper plates and bottles of Coke.

Miki caressed the nape of Pasqualine's neck and

54

kissed it softly. She rubbed her back with eau de Cologne. A cool breeze. She massaged her face with Nivea (protects against irritation due to dry skin) and cream of mallow-flower.

Pasqualine found an old razor, sat on the stool and slowly raised her leg onto the dressing table. She bent her back. The razor traveled slowly toward the top of her thigh. Pasqualine depilated her leg, then bathed it in sixty percent alcohol solution.

Miki stroked Pasqualine's leg displayed upon the pale wood. The cutting edge of the razor made a particular sound.

An ant walked calmly across the mirror, then stopped in the middle. It must have seen its double.

Paper plates scattered around the room. The smell of chicken. Marie-Erna got up to open the window.

"I hate that smell. I don't know how you can eat that stuff."

"You're not hungry enough," Choupette said.

"I'm hungry, but that's no reason to eat junk," Marie-Erna retorted.

"There's nothing good to eat around here anyway," Marie-Flore added.

"I'd eat a man about now," Choupette declared.

"That's all you think about," Marie-Erna complained.

"The pot's calling the kettle black," Choupette shot back.

"I never licked out of your skillet," Marie-Erna challenged.

"And I never shared my bone with another bitch," Choupette had the last word.

"Don't you think it's a little too hot to fight?" Marie-Michèle asked them.

Pasqualine shook it down to the sound of a blood-hot merengue (Shupa Shupa's latest hit). Marie-Erna peppered her with an old Nikon. Pasqualine went on dancing without paying any attention to her routine. The flash illuminated a streaming body.

Papa looked on.

Marie-Flore dozed in an armchair. Miki went to the bathroom to change. She'd spilled brown chicken sauce on the front of her blouse.

A cockroach's black back like a beer-bottle shard. Its fine antennae in constant movement. Papa crushed it with his foot, and it squirted out white pus.

The sun deserted the room. A soft roar rose from the street. The breeze blew away the sour stink of chicken-fried rice.

Dizzy with heat, Choupette crossed the room, wiping her mouth with a Coke-soaked kleenex. She lit herself a cigarette and took a slow drag on it. The room, dark now, the windows closed, pitched like a boat in a child's dream. The tip of her cigarette flared in the darkness.

"Give me a cigarette, Choupette," Miki asked.

"I'm suffocating in here," Pasqualine said, bathed in sweat.

"I'm hungry," Marie-Erna added.

"We should go out," Choupette suggested.

"Shit, can't you relax a minute!" Marie-Michèle complained.

"There's not a damn thing to do here!" Pasqualine cried, wiping her mouth with a paper napkin.

56

"All right, let's go out," Marie-Michèle gave in.

"I don't feel like going any more," Pasqualine declared.

Marie-Michèle practically jumped on her.

"Don't you know what you want?"

"Can't you see she's joking?" Miki said, taking Pasqualine by the waist.

"Are we going out or aren't we?" Choupette demanded. "I'm not going to rot in here."

"Relax," Miki told her, "we're going out."

"Where are we going?" Marie-Flore asked.

"Just *out!*" the girls answered in unison.

The holy night gently lowered its butt upon the city. A drugged sun staggered into the Gulf. Belly to the pavement, the Buick climbed a little ochre hill. Full blast for Tabou Combo's hit (Marie-Erna's favorite group). Papa pretended he was going to change the station. The girls started yelling. The guitar solo grabbed them below the belt. Marie-Erna leaned forward, head against Papa's seat as if someone had just slugged her in the gut. Panting for breath. Wild eyes. The music tormenting her. A fight to the death, no quarter. The singer's scratchy voice straightened her like an uppercut. The body's trance. Ibo rhythms. Erzulia Dahomey. Guinean loas. In a 1957 Buick. Marie-Erna fell back, exhausted. Neck broken. Foam on her lips. The Buick turned at the corner where the Cabane Créole is. The girls laughed and sprinkled perfume and powder on each other. Papa turned around and took a powder-puff in the face. The girls laughed harder. The powder blinded Papa. The Buick drove on, free, with neither driver nor destination. Friday night, baby.

# Gégé, Baby, Your Little Friend Is So Cute

My pulse, alone, like Ibn Lo Bagola
—M. S.-A.

A guy called out to Gégé from down a long passage, right across from the Portail Léogâne. Gégé told me to wait for him while he went to see the guy. A tall thin scarecrow with big starving eyes. Bent at the waist. He and Gégé began talking excitedly. A woman walked by me and looked me up and down.

"Is there anything I can do for you?"

"No, thanks. I'm waiting for a friend."

"Oh, I see." She gave me a knowing smile.

"Here he comes," I said.

She went and wrapped herself around Gégé.

"Gégé, baby, your little friend is so cute. Can I have him for a couple of minutes?"

"We don't have time, Sylvana."

"Just two little minutes. I won't mess him up too much."

"Not tonight."

"If that's the way it is, then go on and never come back, unless you want me to smash your balls to a pulp, you hear me, Gégé? You think you're a man, and you're not even a mouse. Not even a fly. If I wanted to, I could swat you, just like that. I could have your little balls cut off, Gégé!"

We headed out of there, laughing. Gégé gave me a good slap on the back.

"She's from Le Cap."

"Really?"

Gégé looked at me as if I hadn't caught on.

"You know what that means?"

"She was born in Cap Haitien," I stammered.

"Double dunce! Girls from Le Cap fuck better than anyone else in the world."

"The world?"

"The world. And Sylvana was the queen of Le Cap."

"Oh, boy!"

A minute went by.

"What about her getting your balls cut off?"

Gégé started to laugh.

"Don't worry," he told me. "She won't have yours cut off."

"I hope not!"

Gégé kept on laughing.

"She'll cut them off herself, man."

Gégé's laughter howling in the night.

# SCENE VII

# A Game Where Anything Goes

The dance of the tanagra
—M. S.-A.

Doc was practically running with the plates. The restaurant was full and more people were arriving. The musicians from Shupa Shupa were sitting by the front door. They had just finished playing the Rex Theater. The girls, with Papa on their heels, made a grand entrance. The first thing Marie-Erna did was put out her cigarette in the Shupa Shupa guitarist's glass.

"Asshole," Marie-Erna said.

"I had a fever," the guitarist stammered. "I couldn't even drive."

"Find another excuse, asshole. You must think you're hot stuff to stand up someone like me."

"It's true, I had a fever and—"

"You're not good enough to shine my shoes."

Everyone else (musicians and fans) pretended not to listen.

"Tomorrow, no kidding, we can get together at the same place, at the same time, if you like ..."

Marie-Erna gave a fine peal of artificial laughter.

"I must have been crazy or drunk when I said I'd meet you. You're not my type, you're not on my level, and you're not up to my social standing."

The guitarist kept his head down. Marie-Erna slugged him in the back of the neck and went back to her group.

"See you tomorrow," the guitarist said plaintively.

Marie-Erna looked over her shoulder. "Scum like you doesn't deserve a second chance," she spat.

The guitarist raised his head and looked at his friends.

"She sure did have her say," the singer told him with a throaty laugh.

"I said I'd meet her after the gig last Saturday night," the guitarist said. "How did I know Maryse would be there?"

"Was it hard to choose?" asked a young fan sitting at the table.

"Between Maryse and her? No contest, as you can see."

"I understand," the young fan said with a knowing nod. "You really didn't have the choice."

"You think she'll show up tomorrow?" the singer asked with the same throaty laugh.

"Of course," the guitarist said. "You have to understand these girls. If she were really mad, she wouldn't have even looked at me."

"Right," the singer added. "A girl never leaves a man without first taking her vengeance."

"You got it," the guitarist agreed. "You always have to give her a good reason to hate you."

"What about you? Are you going to show up?" the young fan asked.

"Of course," said the guitarist. "To tell her I can't stay."

"Why bother?"

"Because that's exactly what she wants to do to me. Dig this, man: you have to think about what's going on in *her* head."

"What if she doesn't show?" one of the musicians asked.

"She'll show," said the singer confidently. "But she might hide somewhere to see if you're going to show."

"Exactly," the guitarist answered. "And as soon as she sees me, she'll take off. But I'll get there before she does and as soon as she shows, I'll jump out, and bang, I'll tell her I can't stay."

"It's so complicated," the young fan said. "If a girl tells me she wants to see me, no problem, I go."

"The result," said the singer with his eternal throaty laughter, "is that you have no girl."

Hilarity all around.

"It's a tough job," said the guitarist, giving the young fan a slap on the back. "It's no game for amateurs. Girls have gotten more and more demanding."

"But I still don't understand," the young fan insisted. "How can you guys be so sure she'll show?"

"She'll show," said the singer. "That's the way it is."

"But why?"

"She'll show," the guitarist summed up, "because she said she wouldn't."

The young fan shook his head slowly.

# The Rolling Stone Interview

Effect, reflect
—M. S.-A.

An American journalist was taking notes at the musicians' table. He was doing a story for *Rolling Stone* on the new generation of Haitian artists. To his right: a photographer (three cameras around his neck) who was working on a big article on Haiti for *Vogue* (landscape, music, dance, voodoo, the local beauties). Their mandate was different. The *Rolling Stone* journalist was aiming for the heart of things. The photographer stayed on the surface. You have to read both magazines to get the complete picture.

"Without getting into politics," the *Rolling Stone* journalist began, "don't you think this is an odd time for an explosion of new music?"

The guys at the table began laughing like tickled girls.

"Well," said the singer from Shupa Shupa, "it's not

our fault we didn't start earlier."

"The same goes for me," the guitarist added with a laugh. "My father used to say it wasn't a real job because ..."

The singer cut him off.

"My father told me it was a job for people who couldn't do anything else."

The two musicians howled with laughter and slapped themselves on the thighs. The journalist didn't know what to make of his subjects. He let a minute go by before trying to get the discussion back on track.

"I understand," he continued, "it's the same everywhere ... I mean, without talking politics, do you think there's a connection between the country's current economic situation and this veritable explosion of talent in every cultural sector?"

"From the economic point of view," the singer said with a very serious countenance, "my work, I mean, my work with the guys in Shupa Shupa, I mean, my group, *my* work makes it possible for me to eat, and buy some clothes once in a while, and give my mother a little money."

"I just bought myself a car," the guitarist boasted. "It used to belong to Dada Jakaman, the manager of Shleu Shleu."

"Dada gave you a good deal," said the singer, recovering his throaty laughter, "because he wants you for Shleu Shleu."

"You've got it wrong. He's absolutely crazy over one of my cousins. You know Gina?"

"Either you're naïve or you don't know Dada," the singer decided.

64

The journalist felt the interview slipping away. The *Vogue* photographer scanned the room. The place was filled to the rafters. There were practically as many people standing, waiting for a table, as there were sitting down. Doc was running every which way. Everyone wanted him. His was the only restaurant open till five o'clock in the morning.

"Do you think," said the journalist, drawing a fish on a page of his notebook, "that this talent explosion ..."

"You know," said the guitarist, "the word *explosion* is very dangerous in Haiti."

"That word could blow us all away," the singer said without his laugh.

"There's no danger in it for you," the guitarist pointed out. "You're an American. But for us ..."

The journalist looked regretful.

"I'm sorry, I don't want to put you in a difficult situation. But do you think that this upheaval in the cultural sector ..."

The guitarist looked as though he had suddenly been afflicted with a toothache.

"This word *upheaval* ... It's not very kosher either."

The journalist gave an embarrassed smile.

"Actually, the word I had in mind," he said sheepishly, "is *revolution*."

A burst of laughter. The photographer hadn't been following the conversation.

"Do you think," the journalist pressed on, "that all of this is due to the fact that, when all is said and done, Haitian artists refuse to face reality?"

"Excuse me, I have to use the bathroom," said the

65

guitarist.

"And that you turn to art as a kind of escape?"

As he left the table, the guitarist leaned over the singer and whispered in his ear.

"*Blanc sa-a fou nèt ... Chèché oun moyen pour jeté-ou.*"

The journalist waited for an answer that never came.

"What do you think?" he asked.

"I'm not into politics," said the singer. "I only do music."

"I understand," said the *Rolling Stone* journalist, who had finally understood.

The silence was eternal.

"Who's that girl?" the photographer asked suddenly.

"Pasqualine," the singer answered.

"She has something," the photographer said, getting to his feet.

"If I were you, I wouldn't speak to her now," the singer advised.

"Why not?"

"You can never tell how a girl will act when she's in a crowd. Wait till she's alone."

But the photographer was already at Pasqualine's table.

## SCENE IX

# How to Get a Table at Doc's

The babble of the ball
—M. S.-A.

"Have you ever heard of *Vogue?*" asked the photographer in his thick New York accent.

"No," replied Pasqualine, lowering her eyes like a young virgin in an Italian movie.

"What? You've never heard of *Vogue?* You know, the fashion magazine."

"I answered that question." She had her claws out already. "Why should I have heard of *Vogue?*"

"You're so beautiful."

The girls burst out laughing, their breasts thrust forward and their rear ends in motion. A bad sign.

"I'm talking professionally here. I'm a photographer for *Vogue.* I've been everywhere, and I've noticed that girls like you read *Vogue.* It's the most important fashion magazine

67

in the world."

"So what?" Pasqualine asked.

"So what?" Choupette answered her. "It's obvious. He wants to screw you in the name of *Vogue*."

"That's what it all comes down to," Marie-Erna lamented in a reed-thin voice.

The photographer blushed beet-red.

"It's not what you think," he stammered.

"Hey," Choupette interrupted him, "I bet that's how you get all your girls."

"Just by saying *Vogue*," Marie-Flore added.

"Does it work every time?" Miki inquired.

Choupette slid her way slowly toward the photographer and grabbed his balls in her right hand.

"Would it work if I said *Vogue?*"

The photographer drew a flimsy paper napkin from his left back pocket and wiped his forehead.

"Why won't it work for me if I say *Vogue?*" Choupette complained with stagy sadness.

"You don't understand," said Marie-Erna with a laugh. She pointed a finger at the photographer. "It only works if he says *Vogue*."

"Hey, Mr. Vogue, don't leave," Miki pleaded through her laughter.

"You scared him off," Marie-Michèle said. "He wasn't that bad."

"I know you, you've got to have them all," Choupette answered cuttingly.

Marie-Michèle leapt at Choupette. Miki caught her as she flew by.

"You've got no right to say that to *me*, Choupette.

68

Someone else, maybe, but not you. You're always giving everyone the eye."

"Maybe so, but I don't play your intellectual games. Your little game won't work with me. You act so high and mighty every time we try and have a little fun, but you're the biggest slut in town."

Marie-Michèle's shocked face. The others didn't move a muscle.

"What did I say wrong? What did I do wrong? All I said was that he was cute and that you scared him off, and now suddenly I don't have the right to say ..."

"I'm hungry," Marie-Erna decided.

Doc arrived, sweating.

"What's the matter? Why don't you sit down?"

"There's no room," Marie-Michèle said.

Doc scanned the room. It was full to the rafters.

"The restaurant is full," he moaned.

"I noticed," said Marie-Michèle in her most snobbish voice.

"So what'll it be?" Doc asked anxiously, his eyes darting right and left in case someone needed him elsewhere.

"This place has got no class," said Marie-Erna.

"We've been waiting for a table forever, Doc," Miki put in.

"If you don't want us, we can always go elsewhere," Choupette said.

"Everything is closed around here this time of night," Doc answered coolly.

"Don't tempt us, Doc," Miki replied. "You know we would open a restaurant across the road and go there if we felt like it. Then we'd see who'd come out on top. Your memory's gotten short, Doc. You forgot we're the ones who put your restaurant on the map."

"Before," Choupette chimed in, "nobody but *tap-tap* drivers came into your joint."

"What can I do?" Doc asked nervously.

"Give us that table," Marie-Michèle told him.

Doc stared at her in disbelief.

"Can't you see there's already someone sitting there?"

"I noticed."

That was Marie-Michèle's favorite expression.

"So?"

"So what?" Marie-Michèle said softly.

"Take another table. I'll look after it."

"No way. You want to put us next to the kitchen. I don't want to smell like fried oil for the rest of the night."

"What can I do? He's a good customer. Besides, he's with his wife."

"I can ask him for the table," said Marie-Michèle, who had decided to settle things in her discreet but effective way.

"You go ahead, but I can't do it," Doc told her.

Marie-Michèle danced her way toward the table. Her long legs had a lot to do with her gazelle look. She leaned over the man, who was sitting across from a heavily made-up woman with expensive jewelry hanging off every part of her body (arms, neck, ears), and whispered something into his ear. Her eyes never left his wife's face. Immediately, the woman gave her husband a stinging slap and both of them left the restaurant. Coolly, Marie-Michèle went back to her friends. Doc threw his rag on the floor.

70

"They left without paying! You're going to have to settle up!"

Papa took out his wallet and made Doc smile again.

"What did you say to him?" Choupette asked eagerly.

"I asked him if she was the bitch he was two-timing me with."

# I Cried When I Saw *Le Rebelle* with Amalia Mendoza

Under the halo of my lament
—M. S.-A.

The last show at the Olympia had finished. People were streaming out of the movie house in tears. An enormous poster sat on the sidewalk: *Le Rebelle* with Amalia Mendoza. We all loved it when the handsome gypsy says, "He who dances with Soledad will die." I saw the film with my mother and Aunt Renée. They cried. So did I. Since I'm the only male in the house, whenever one of my aunts wants to go to the movies, I have to go with her. I saw *Le Rebelle* at least four times. The last time I didn't cry. I would never tell Gégé I cried even once.

"I don't get it why people cry when they go to the movies," Gégé said, spitting on the ground.

"Maybe they're sensitive," I risked the comment.

Gégé shot me a look.

"Damn it!" he shouted. "Don't they know it's only a movie? After all, they bought a ticket for it."

"Sometimes people forget if they're really caught up in the story."

Gégé laughed. "They can't fool me. I never cry."

We said nothing. From the distance came the voice of Sylvana, the girl from Le Cap, who cuts off men's balls. Suddenly, Gégé turned to me.

"What about you?"

"What about me?"

"Do you cry?"

A guitar played Soledad's song from the end of long, dark passage.

"Are you afraid to answer me?"

"I never cry, Gégé."

"That's what I thought," he said seriously.

Women were streaming onto the street, dressed like fairytale princesses. Most of the men were in white, and they wore hats.

"Are they going to a party?" I asked Gégé.

"It's always like that down here."

"Even during the week?"

"Every day."

Suddenly, the Portail put on a different face. The world of the night flowed onto the sidewalk. The brush of silk. The heavy perfume of *ilang-ilang*.

The night was young.

SCENE XI

# A Shark at the Macaya Bar

These beasts all sated with blood
—M. S.-A.

It was starting to get really late. Gégé was waiting for me
to ask him to walk me home. That's his way of humiliat-
ing me. My mother must be worried. I didn't know how
long I could play his little game. I decided to wait a little
longer. Then we'd see. We crossed the main road, slipping
between the *tap-taps*, the ambulance sirens (always loudest
on Friday nights), the hysterical taxi horns and the dense
crowds that blocked the sidewalk. It was like a riot. Gégé
was far ahead of me. All the way to the Macaya Bar. The
girls were sitting on the front steps. Mostly Dominicans,
with three or four Haitians, all made up and ready to face
the night. Fever. Merengue. The mad desire of the hatted
men. Gégé knew a waiter at the Macaya Bar. Johnny had
quit school two years ago to take the job. What do you

74

expect, he spent more time at the bar than in the class-
room. Sometimes he gave Gégé tips about the whores.
Who was going with whom. You had to be careful! Once
a whore hooks up with a shark (that's what Gégé calls the
Tontons Macoutes), you have to clear the decks, and fast.
Gégé wasn't afraid of the sharks. He was the only person I
knew who wasn't. Everyone's afraid of the sharks. Little
sharks are afraid of big ones. And big ones fear the bigger.
Sharks feed on each other, but first they devour non-
sharks. That's the way they are. But Gégé wasn't afraid of
them. Gégé went to see Johnny in the back, in the little
room next to the toilet. I stayed out on the sidewalk,
under the big coral tree, not too far from the whores, but
not too close either. I shivered with desire and stole a
glance at them. What breasts! If only I could weigh them
gently in my hand, then take each one in my mouth! Why
couldn't I be that fat pig smothering that yellow flame in
her tiny yellow silk dress? The devil's own merengue. Red
everywhere. Mouths, cheeks, nails. Red. Red. Red. A
whore stood up to get a cold drink, or so I thought. She
turned her back, shot me a look from over her shoulder,
then shook her rear end like it was on fire. Sometimes I
wonder if God exists, and if he does, why he gave such
power to a pair of buttocks.

"Hey, you, kid, come here," a big shark growled at
me. He was standing right next to me, and I hadn't even
noticed.

I took a step in his direction.

"You want a drink?" he asked.

The girl sitting next to him (thin body in a tight
dress, the kind fat pigs like) stepped in.

"Go away, you've got no business here."

"Wait a minute!" the shark burst out. "You're being rude to my guest."

Something was happening; I tried to figure out what. The whore jumped to her feet.

"Get out of here, I'm warning you."

I hesitated. My limbs were made of lead.

"Run, kid, run!" the thin girl in the red dress shouted hysterically.

I started running. My legs reacted slowly. I got a bad start. I didn't know why I was running. What was happening, what was so dangerous? Something was up. Where should I go? I ran towards the crowd. Nobody paid any attention; the usual occurrence in this part of town. I glanced back a second and saw the barrel of a .38 pointed at me. I threw myself down the little ravine by the Portail Léogâne police station. A policeman came out on the front step and waved happily to the shark who still had his .38 aimed at my back.

"Don't worry," the policeman told me. "He's drunk as a skunk. He couldn't shoot you if he tried."

I kept on running.

"He couldn't hit an elephant in a hallway!" the policeman shouted.

I was running through molasses. I heard the policeman laughing. I pushed my way through the crowd, then looked back: the .38 was still pointing at me. Finally I got out of range and went to wait for Gégé near the Stadium.

The match was just ending. Don Bosco had crushed Bacardi five to nothing.

# It's Crazy, But I Think He's Cute

Far from the gods weary of this dance
—M. S.-A.

"Bring me more chicken, Doc. What are you waiting for?" Choupette cried.

"For you to pay," Doc called back from the kitchen.

"In kind?" asked Marie-Erna.

"I need cold cash," he answered as he came in with the plates.

"What's the matter, are you impotent or something?" said Choupette, grabbing for Doc's balls.

"I don't know what you see in chicken," Marie-Erna whined.

"The same thing you see in sex," Choupette shut her up.

"Why are you two always fighting?"

77

"Maybe they've got the same man," Marie-Michèle offered, then looked up at the ceiling.

"Me?" said Marie-Erna, putting on a look of disgust.

"Laugh if you like," Choupette put in, "but I hate promiscuity. I never share anything with anybody."

Pasqualine began to stretch, exposing the light down under her arms. So much for Marie-Erna's rejoinder.

"I don't want to hang around here ... I'm going to the beach bright and early tomorrow," said Pasqualine languorously.

"Early for you means noon," Marie-Flore scoffed.

"I'm going to sleep at your house, Miki," Pasqualine told her. "I won't have time to go up to Pétionville."

"What's so special about you, Pasqualine?" Choupette wanted to know. "Everybody's going to the beach tomorrow."

"Maybe. But I'm not going with you."

"We're going with Papa!" Marie-Flore cried happily.

Papa smiled sadly.

"I can't ... I have to take my wife and kids to La Plaine," he whimpered.

"Oh, no, Papa! You took them somewhere three weeks ago," Choupette complained. "What's come over you?"

"You're getting old, Papa," Marie-Flore warned him.

"There's no more lead in his pencil," Choupette cackled.

"Don't push it, Choupette," Marie-Michèle said quietly.

"Shit," Choupette protested, "I try and find something interesting to do tomorrow, and you tell me I'm

78

exaggerating ... Somebody tell me what I'm exaggerating about!"

"Don't you think it's normal, Choupette, for him to take his family out once in a while?"

Choupette looked at Marie-Michèle with wide eyes, then smiled. She'd just picked up the hidden message.

"That's true, Papa. You should spend more time with your family."

"Ask Doc to fix you up a doggy bag for your wife," Marie-Michèle upped the ante.

"Good idea," Choupette said, full of sweetness. "It's always appreciated ... Don't worry about us, we'll find some way of getting to the beach tomorrow."

"If you think you can," Papa murmured.

Gently, Choupette stroked his cheek.

"Of course. We'll ask Pasqualine's friend to take us. Aren't you going to the beach with your boyfriend, Pasqua?"

"I told you, Choupette. Frank is supposed to get me at Miki's tomorrow at noon."

"We'll go with you if it's okay with Frank," Choupette said.

"It's not up to Frank," Pasqualine shot back. "I have other plans."

"Oh, well, if you can't do it," Marie-Erna said, "I can always ask Peddy."

"Peddy? The singer for Shleu Shleu? Not him! If Peddy comes, then the rest of the band will, too, and those guys can't keep their hands off my tits, and that bugs my ass."

"Hey, Marie-Flore," said Marie-Erna with a half-smile, "you didn't seem to mind the last time."

79

"Just because I liked something once doesn't mean I want to do it again."

Suddenly, Papa got the picture.

"All right," he said, "I'll take you to the beach tomorrow after all."

"What about your family?" the girls asked in unison.

"Next Saturday," Papa resolved.

"It won't be our fault if your wife doesn't go to La Plaine tomorrow."

"Stop it, Choupette," Marie-Michèle whispered. "You always go too far."

"I want him to beg."

"You won, Choupette. He said he wouldn't take out his wife."

"That's not enough," she hissed. "I never want him to mention her name again."

"Shit, Choupette, leave him alone already," said Marie-Michèle.

"Okay. But it's the last time ..."

Papa finished off his chicken. Marie-Flore fixed her breasts; they were starting to pop out of her bra.

"Mother of God," Marie-Michèle wondered, shooting a quick look at Papa. "What did he ever do to you?"

"I hate men who've got no guts," said Choupette.

"It's crazy, but I think he's cute," Marie-Michèle said softly.

## SCENE XIII

# The Tiger Stalks the Tropical Night

Eternal ashes of blind skin
—M. S.-A.

A guy in a Panama hat and a white suit that was too tight for him accosted me.

"You see the Tiger?"

"No."

I didn't know the Tiger, but Gégé told me never to admit not knowing something, especially in the red zone.

"Shit, the bastard's never there when you need him."

Furious, the man looked around. I saw how dirty his suit was.

"What are you doing?"

"Nothing," I answered.

"Nothing?"

"I'm waiting for somebody."

"Oh … You are?" he said.

There was a pause.

"Is it for a job?"

"No," I replied. "I'm waiting for a friend."

"You're not working tonight?"

"No."

"Then can you help me out? I've got three tourists on my hands. They're already drunk. Just give them a little suck."

"Not tonight," I said.

He looked at me furiously.

"You told me you weren't working tonight. It's just a little blow job, for Christ's sake … If I lose these guys, the whole boat'll know, and my weekend's shot. I'll make it worth your while."

"No."

He was about to explode.

"Name your price, shit, go ahead, bleed me dry. You're all the same. I'll give you three times the usual price."

"No," I said to see how far he'd go.

"Just tell me what you want!"

"Nothing."

"Nothing?"

"Yes. Nothing."

He stared at me with his rheumy eyes.

"What does that mean, 'nothing?'"

"I don't want anything," I said, unshakeable.

"Tell me your price, shit."

"No."

"No, what?" he finally exploded. "You're working for

the police. Well, I am, too."

"Here comes my friend," I said coolly.

"What's going on?" Gégé asked.

"This guy wants me to take on his three sailors."

"Can't you suck them off yourself?" Gégé suggested.

We left the guy, still searching far and wide, in hopes that the Tiger would spring from the tropical night.

SCENE XIV

# The Only Good Shark Is a Castrated Shark

Widowed of vain care
—M. S.-A.

Gégé was furious at the shark. I wanted to go home, but he had other ideas. He wanted us to go back to the Macaya Bar. I tried to convince him that the shark was drunk, that he couldn't have hit me. Gégé wouldn't leave it alone. We had to settle the score. We went back towards the whorehouse, following a group of Don Bosco fans who wanted to party at the little bar by the police station.

Gégé told me to wait for him outside and start running towards the Bicentenaire (the street that borders the sea) as soon as I heard a scream. He went into the whorehouse. I saw him talking to Johnny. It looked like Johnny wasn't going for it. He waved his hands in the air, he refused. Gégé kept up. What were they discussing, what were they plotting? Finally, Johnny gave in. He handed Gégé something wrapped in a handkerchief. Gégé moved off. Johnny tried to hold him back. They started talking again. Suddenly, Gégé headed for the wooden staircase and I lost sight of him. I didn't have to wait long. A terrible scream shook the Macaya. All the lights in the upstairs rooms went on at once. Gégé came running out of the bar and caught up with me.

"Quick, along the tracks!"

I ran. Gégé ran. A jeep was following us. We slipped behind the power plant. Gégé told me to watch out for the cables lying on the ground. The jeep couldn't follow us in there. I stayed close to Gégé because I didn't know the area. Now and then we heard the siren from the Haitian Sugar Company. A slow train passed with its heavy load of cane. Gégé darted between two cars. I did the same. We headed toward the King Solomon Star, the biggest whoring hotel in Port-au-Prince, where Gégé knew a top-level shark. The barman told us he'd be there later. We couldn't wait. A prostitute in a wedding dress latched onto Gégé.

"Tonight is our wedding night," she told him.

"Another time, Philomena."

We crossed the big lobby on the run. I asked Gégé who the woman was.

"She's crazy," he said.

He told me her fiancé forgot to show up at their wedding. Ever since, she's been marrying a different man every night. We kept on running all the way to the place Sainte-Anne. I figured out where we were. I used to come here to fight the students from the Lycée Toussaint. The square was poorly lit. That served us well. We sat down on a bench to catch our breath in the overwhelming scent of jasmine.

"What did you do to that shark, Gégé?"

"I cut off his balls."

"What?"

"I cut off the bastard's balls while he was sleeping off his rum."

"You're crazy! That's impossible! That's not true! You didn't do that! You lost your mind! You've gone completely crazy!"

"It's like I'm telling you ..."

"I don't believe you," I told him, though I knew Gégé could very well have done it.

Gégé opened his bloody hands and a piece of flesh dropped to the ground. I was dumbstruck. Gégé picked up the bleeding piece of meat.

"I think I'll hold onto them," he said.

# Women on the Verge of a
# Nervous Breakdown

On the loins of your dark despair, Mathsheba
—M. S.-A.

I didn't go home last night. I was too afraid. The sharks
were sure to know where I lived. They'd come and get me
in their DKWs. Gégé was luckier. No one knew where his
house was. Not even me. Maybe he didn't even have one.
It's better when you don't have an address. You can do anything you want, then disappear into the night, never to be
heard from again. I'd give anything to be in Gégé's shoes.
He did the damage, but I was the one the sharks were
after. They'd remember me. They'd think I'd done it out
of vengeance. They'd start by cutting my balls off. Maybe
I'd even have to eat them. Gégé would lie low a month or
two, then return to an enthusiastic reception. Meanwhile,
I'd be a moldering corpse, even if I'd done everything in

my power to keep Gégé from going back to the Macaya and cutting the shark. The shark might have been drunk when he pointed his .38 at me, but the thin girl with the black hair could identify me. She was a good girl. She saved my life once. But if she ever had to choose between her life and mine, I knew which way she'd go.

My mother must have been worried sick, considering what time it was. I pictured her pacing the room. Aunt Renée would be wringing her hands, filling the air with her great sighs.

"Stop that, Renée," said Aunt Raymonde, who had taken control of the operation. "You're making me dizzy."

Aunt Renée stopped her sighing for a minute but wrung her hands twice as hard.

"It's the first time he's ever done this," my mother said.

"Well, there's a first time for everything," said Aunt Raymonde.

"But, Raymonde," my mother said, sobbing, "he's only a child."

"He's a man, Marie. Maybe he's already a father. When are you going to open your eyes in this house?"

"He's not a man," said Aunt Renée with all the strength in her body. "*There's no man in this house!*"

Aunt Ninine appeared in the doorway.

"What's going on here?" she asked.

"He hasn't come home," Aunt Renée told her. "Maybe he never will."

Aunt Renée started pacing again, sighing more heavily and wringing her hands more desperately.

"Renée, for the love of God, would you stop?" Aunt Raymonde said.

"What are we going to do about it?" asked Aunt Gilberte, who loved action.

"We're not going to do anything," answered Aunt Raymonde, who wanted to frighten my mother.

"How can you say that?" my mother said in disbelief.

"We're not going to panic. We're going to wait until he comes back from the whorehouse," Aunt Raymonde declared.

"The whorehouse!" my mother and Aunt Gilberte cried in unison.

"What's a whorehouse?" Aunt Renée wanted to know. "Nobody ever tells me anything."

"If it's the first time," Aunt Ninine spoke, "he won't come back before noon."

"Why not?" Aunt Renée asked. "What's he going to do there that will take all that time?"

"What he does there is none of our business," Aunt Raymonde said, tight-lipped.

"It's the only thing he can't do here," Aunt Ninine said with a laugh.

My mother shot her a disapproving look.

"Why won't anyone tell me what this whorehouse business is?" Aunt Renée lamented.

"If you want to go to heaven, you have to die first," Aunt Ninine spoke softly.

Suddenly Aunt Renée went pale.

"You're keeping something from me," she said, sick with worry.

"Don't trouble yourself, Renée, it won't kill him," Aunt Ninine said with a smile.

"What's everyone talking about?" she demanded,

more alarmed than ever. "Who died?"

"That's enough, Renée," Raymonde ordered her. "You have nothing to do with this."

"It's the first time he's ever done such a thing," my mother said in a broken voice.

"What do we do?" Aunt Gilberte asked.

"I told you, we can't do anything before noon," Aunt Ninine repeated.

"What's so special about noon?" Aunt Renée asked again.

"Because," Aunt Ninine articulated slowly, " the prostitutes never get up before noon."

Aunt Renée put her hand to her mouth and hurried out of the room.

SCENE XVI

# Two Will-o'-the-Wisps

Into the spider's fractured web
—M. S.-A.

I was at Miki's house. The only place where I'd be safe. Miki knew all the sharks. No one would ever dream of looking for me here. Miki was fast asleep when I knocked on her door.

"Who is it?" she asked sleepily.

"Me."

She opened up immediately. You could see she was used to opening her door for people.

"What are you doing here?"

"Can I come in?"

She let me in.

"Don't you know what time it is?" she asked with a little smile.

"I have to hide."

"What's the matter?"

Her voice sounded a little worried but not *too* worried.

"The sharks."

"What about them?"

Miki was one of the few people in this town who didn't panic at the word *shark*.

"They're looking for me," I told her.

She hesitated half a second.

"Okay," she said. "You can tell me about it tomorrow."

I followed her to her room. She gave me a sheet and pillow. I went and lay down on the living-room sofa.

Sleep came quickly. I dreamed I was falling into a bottomless pit.


"Oh, you scared me," said a woman's voice.

Pasqualine came in. I'd never seen her up close. She was even hotter in the flesh than the way she looked from my window. Getting near her was like trying to put out a fire with gasoline. She must have been about my age. Fairly tall, with black, very black hair, red lips and light skin. And nothing but a towel around her waist. Small, pretty breasts. I watched her from the corner of one eye. Already my sex was on the rise. My balls ached. I had to piss, and then this girl. Too close for comfort. The tips of my breasts hurt. If she didn't go away pretty soon, I'd have an ejaculation right then and there.

"Excuse me," I managed to murmur, "didn't Miki tell you?"

"What was she supposed to tell me?" Pasqualine asked, a smile playing at her lips.

She didn't seem the least embarrassed at being half-naked. Miki came out and kissed her on the shoulder.

"Don't worry, Pasqua, he's the boy from across the road. He'll be staying here a while."

"I'm not worried," Pasqualine answered casually. "Why would I be worried?"

"It's just something you say," Miki told her, then began looking for a record in the big mahogany cabinet.

I tried to get dressed under the sheet. The sun was shining behind the Venetian blinds. It must have been eleven o'clock. Miki put on a Tabou record.

"Do you like them?" she asked me.

"A lot," I said. "They're my favorite group."

"Good for you," Miki answered. "I can't stand them. I can't imagine what people see in them."

"Why are you playing it?"

"Pasqualine likes them."

Miki was twenty years old, or almost. The house wasn't really hers. It belonged to a businessman who stopped by from time to time, once every couple months. When he was there, Miki turned into a serious young lady. She put nothing but Vivaldi's *Four Seasons* on the record player, and forgot about her girlfriends. The businessman took her to fancy restaurants (the Rond-Point or the Hippopotamus), and sometimes to receptions at the National Palace. I could scarcely recognize her in an evening dress, though she was as beautiful in a dress as in jeans. When the businessman left, the party began again. The girls came streaming back. Cars pulled up in front of the house and honked their horns, day and night.

"What happened last night?" Miki asked as she sorted through her records.

"You want to know everything that happened?"

"Actually, I don't have the time. I'm going to the beach, and I've got loads of things to do."

"Then I'll make it snappy. Last night, we were at the Macaya Bar, and Gégé cut off a shark's balls."

Miki stood stock still a moment.

"Can you start over again?"

"Last night, Gégé cut off a shark's balls."

"Who's Gégé?"

"A friend."

"If you didn't do it, why do you have to hide?"

"The shark wanted to shoot me."

"I see … When you say that he cut off his balls, what exactly do you mean?"

"I mean, Miki, that he cut off his balls."

"Why did he do that?"

"Gégé is very impulsive."

"That hurts a lot, you know," Miki laughed.

She was about to say something else when Pasqualine called from the bathroom.

"Can you come and wash my back, Miki?"

"Of course, *ma belle*."

Miki went off with a laugh. Cruel laughter. Gégé's laughter.

## SCENE XVII

# Hands Off My Breasts, Frank!

Angélique and Milady's frozen smile
—M. S.-A.

Pasqualine and Miki were in the bathroom. I have sensitive ears. I heard the water running, then squeals of laughter. I was lying on my back. Suddenly a guy came bursting into the room.

He looked at me suspiciously. I'd seen him before.

"Where's Pasqualine?"

"In the bathroom," I said.

He must have been in his fifties. Still well muscled, bald, piercing eyes and a strangler's hands.

"Do you want me to tell her you're here?"

He gave me a terrifying look.

"Who are you?"

Without hesitating, or almost, I told him, "Miki's little brother."

95

"I never saw you before," he said angrily.

"I wasn't here before. I came last night."

He didn't answer. His face was tight, his fists clenched. One punch and it was my funeral.

"I'll go tell them," I offered.

I ran off to the bathroom and knocked on the door. Miki opened up.

"There's a guy waiting for Pasqualine in the living-room. Come quick before he strangles me."

"What guy?" Pasqualine asked with a frown.

"He looks like a killer to me."

Miki burst out laughing.

"It must be Frank."

"He won't hurt a fly if I don't tell him to," Pasqualine assured me.

"He's a born killer," Miki added. "If Pasqualine told him to, he'd strangle half this town."

"That's what I figured," I said.

They went on laughing, especially Pasqualine, with that throaty laughter so full of promised pleasures.

"Don't worry," Miki advised. "When Pasqualine's around, he's as gentle as a lamb."

"I'm not worried ... What should I tell the killer?"

"Tell him to wait."

"Don't tell him anything," Pasqualine corrected her. "He'll just wait, that's all."

I decided to tell him to wait a little longer in the most polite voice I could muster. I wondered how a fifteen-year-old girl could have tamed such a monster. Her breasts. Her contemptuous little pout. Her pink tongue that slipped between her lips like a sturgeon pulled from water. The

96

long curve of her back. Her red nails. Weapons as terrible as big biceps and a square jaw. Pasqualine could bat an eyelash and a man (any man, regardless of race, color or creed) would fall dead at her feet. The other eyelash would bring him back to life.

"Hey, Miki," I said after knocking on the door, "I told him I was your brother."

"Okay, baby brother, I get the picture."

Frank paced the room. I tried to take up as little space as possible. I wouldn't want to be in the torture chamber with him. Oh, boy, that must hurt. Hurt me, Frank, hurt me harder. I picked up a book lying on the floor. Poetry by Magloire Saint-Aude. Miki reads Saint-Aude. I didn't know that. I love Saint-Aude. I was willing to love anyone who loved Saint-Aude. I've never told anyone that I like poetry. Gégé hates it. He says only girls and guys who aren't getting any like it. Funny, the girls I know would rather listen to music than read poetry. The two aren't necessarily the same. There's always a bit of music in a good poem, but no one can claim there's always poetry in a song.

I didn't know Miki read Saint-Aude. The only poet worthy of the name in this country where everyone thinks he's a poet. I opened Saint-Aude's book, then closed it immediately. Frank was staring at me from the middle of the room. I read contempt in his eyes. Suddenly I was nauseous with fear. He must know everything that happened last night. He must be friends with the shark who got his balls cut off by Gégé. He'd take me to Fort Dimanche, the terrible prison by the sea. They don't even have to torture you there. They just let you rot away. The cells are below sea level, and every time the tide comes in, the prisoners drown in the mud from the bottom of the bay. That's where the big grey garbage trucks dump the city's trash. Maybe they had other plans for me. Like cooking me over a slow fire. Or forcing me to eat my excrement. Or having me sodomized by a hundred prisoners starving for fresh meat. The worst thing is knowing that reality is more abominable than anything I could dream up. Frank was staring at me intently, as if trying to remember something. Then he put his hand to his forehead and ran down the hallway to the bathroom. I heard Pasqualine shrieking. The fear of the lion-tamer faced with an animal that has become uncontrollable.

"Hands off my breasts, Frank!"

All hell broke loose. Afterwards, silence. A silence full of unspoken words. I picked up my book. The sun continued its slow progress across the floor. It would reach the sofa around noon, in less than half an hour. Suddenly, I heard Pasqualine's high-pitched cry, followed by a heavy, dull death-rattle that must have come from Frank. Who else could it have been?

I heard Miki's voice.

"That's enough … We'd better go now, otherwise there won't be anything left to eat out there."

Ten minutes later, Pasqualine swept past me, as fresh as a wild rose after a rain. Frank followed her, his legs a little shaky.

Miki stopped at the door.

"Take good care of the house, baby brother," she called out with a conspiratorial smile.

A smile barely visible to the naked eye.

98

# Neither Lord Nor Master

> Accept this offering of necklaces,
> my mournful fandango
> —M. S.-A.

The sun reached the sofa. I picked up Saint-Aude's poetry and read:

> In the bard's tent
> sleeps the gold of my lamp.

I closed the book and sat in motionless meditation. My senses open. I wanted the air to yield up the multiple meanings of these lines. A good line of poetry lives at room temperature. You begin by conjuring up its special smell that fills your being. The smell of the poet when he wrote the line. In this case, the line smells of cat piss, lime and human salt. Its taste is that of the Host, bread without leavening. A good line will burn your fingers. Its average speed is three hundred and sixty kilometers an hour. You don't need more than one good line a day.

I got up to make a sandwich in the kitchen. Miki had fixed me a bowl of chocolate. The girls' underwear was scattered through the house.

I went to wash my face in the sink. The combined smell of perfume, sweat and sperm almost knocked me off my feet. I lingered there a minute or two to breathe it all in.

Outside, a car horn sounded a dozen times. I wanted to tell them that everyone was gone, and that they'd all headed for the beach. I stopped; I'd almost forgotten I was a wanted man. Where could Gégé be? No doubt cooking up some new trouble. Knowing him, he was probably on a fresh scent. He would change shirts, and no one would know who he was. Gégé was always on the move. It's hard to hit a moving target. Meanwhile, I was waiting here, nailed to the spot, waiting like a fool for them to come and pick me up. Like a cow hiding in a slaughterhouse. Maybe that *was* the right place to hide. No one would ever think of looking for a cow in a slaughterhouse. Sharks come and go at Miki's place and never even look at me.

"Where's Miki?" Choupette asked abruptly as she stormed into the house.

I knew all of them. They didn't know who I was, but I'd seen them plenty of times, in every possible position. I can see everything in Miki's house from my window.

"She left."

The other girls came in behind Choupette. Papa must have stayed in the car.

"Miki went to the beach with Pasqualine," I repeated.

100

Marie-Erna waved her hand in the air as if to say she knew that and didn't give a damn. The girls fanned out through the house. They took everything: clothes, food, perfume, records, a bottle of Chanel No. 5 and Cover Girl make-up. A regular raid. I couldn't do anything about it. I didn't know the code. Miki had asked me to look after the house, but what did she really mean? Was she serious? Had she anticipated this horde of pillagers? Was this the normal thing to do? What was really going on? Miki was their friend, wasn't she? But these girls would devour anyone—including each other.

A fight broke out over a scarf.

"Keep you hands off that," Choupette ordered.

"How come?" Marie-Erna asked.

"It belongs to me, shit. I lent it to Miki last week."

"I don't believe you," said Marie-Erna and put the scarf in her black leather purse.

"Give it to me!" Choupette raged.

"Hey, girls, calm down," said Papa, who had just walked into the room.

"Shut your face," Choupette shot back, turning on him.

Papa cut a quick look in my direction. I didn't lower my eyes. He wasn't Frank, after all.

"You're a real bitch," Marie-Erna told Choupette.

I watched the tennis game. Balls were flying over the net from both sides. Smashes from all corners. Real professionals. Papa wouldn't be asked to umpire. Marie-Erna was sexier than Choupette, in a certain way. Though I was probably the only one who held that opinion. Choupette was so absolutely physical. Her mere presence was enough

101

to make you surrender. When you saw her, you could think of only one thing. Her mouth was made for it. Her lips, her teeth (glistening white), her wrists, her ankles, everything about her was designed to push men (and women, too) to the edge of despair, madness and murder. Marie-Erna was more subtle. When you first cast your eyes on her, she seemed almost ordinary. But one look and you were caught, hopelessly trapped. With Pasqualine as their princess, these girls were the *crème de la crème* of man-killers in this town.

"All right, you can have it," Marie-Erna said, this time, about a blouse.

"No, you keep it," Choupette said casually. "I don't want it any more."

"I don't want it either," Marie-Erna told her. "I don't really like Miki's stuff."

Choupette took the blouse from Marie-Erna's hands and threw it on top of the record player.

"Come on, let's go," she ordered.

"If you don't really need it, then I think I will take it," Marie-Erna decided, stuffing the blouse into her bag.

"You're a walking garbage can," Choupette told her.

Papa got to his feet. Did he understand the girls' secret code? I didn't think so. He was only following along. But then again, you never know.

"Let's go, Marie-Michèle," Choupette called out.

Marie-Michèle had stayed by the window the entire time, not moving, with her backed turned. Obviously, she didn't agree with the proceedings.

"Go on without me," she said through tight lips.

"Come on," Marie-Erna urged, "it'll be fun out

there."

"No. I don't feel like it any more."

"Leave her alone," said Choupette, "we're going to have a ball without her."

"That's right, go ahead and have fun," said Marie-Michèle.

"Come on," Marie-Erna begged from the door.

"Don't worry about me ... I'm having my period."

"So what?"

"I just started, and I hate the smell of blood on me."

"Bye-bye," said Choupette drily.

The two girls went out, making the most of their departure. Papa followed behind.

"I'm sure she's got something going," Choupette said.

"That bitch!" Marie-Erna agreed.

The Buick pulled off in a cloud of dust. The beach was less than an hour away.

SCENE XIX

# The Rules of the Game

My eyes, this rotten paste
—M. S.-A.

Marie-Michèle was still at the window, though her friends had long since left. She looked lost. I watched her in her blue dress. Obviously, she had a lot more class than the others (except Miki), but there was still something hard in her face. A scar ran down her left cheek. Suddenly, she turned and sprung.

"I hate them sometimes."

"Who?" I asked, though I knew the answer.

She shot a look towards the door.

"They're your friends."

"Yes," she said under her breath. "Yes and no ... they're not really friends."

"I see."

She turned back to the window, still angry. I studied

the gracious line of her ankles.

"I'm in med school," she told me in a hoarse voice.

I didn't understand, and she saw that in my eyes.

"I'm studying medicine. I'm in second year."

"I see."

"I'm here because of Miki ..."

"Miki's great."

She smiled.

"She is. The rest of them are just leeches. Little bitches. I don't understand what Miki sees in them."

Every one of those girls would have said the same thing about the others. Marie-Michèle broke her fingernail. She pulled off the broken nail and made a face.

A poster of a Gauguin painting hung on the wall, just behind her head. A brightly colored canvas from his Tahiti period. Two girls, one bare-breasted. She is holding something that looks like a little basket of fruit. Her breasts are firm. The face of a natural beauty, without false modesty. The pleasure of being alive. People have always confused Haiti and Tahiti.

"Who are you anyway?" Marie-Michèle turned and asked.

"I live across the street. You can see my room from here."

She glanced out the window, then turned back with a teasing smile.

"You can see everything that goes on in here."

"That's possible," I admitted.

"I'm sure you make good use of the view."

"Not that much."

She looked at me and shook her head slowly. Her fine-boned face changed quickly from sadness to joy, without warning. She looked like someone who's been keeping a secret so well that even she forgot it. She darted into the hallway and a second later I heard her dialing the phone.

Marie-Michèle spoke softly into the receiver. Her voice was urgent, a little anxious. I paid no attention. I was waiting for her to come back and continue the conversation. Boredom had fallen upon me like a weight. Like the blade of a guillotine. I was bored to death. I couldn't stay here and do nothing. I had to move. But I couldn't leave. I stared into the emptiness and thought of nothing. I opened Magloire Saint-Aude's book. A page at random. I read:

> The prisoner's poem
> As memory's sun sinks.

That's crazy! I came to this place and found a book that expressed my emotions perfectly, what I was feeling at that very instant. A poem touches us when it speaks specifically of our state of mind at the moment we read it. Sunlight through a window can't replace the real sun. The sun is outside, and I'm in here. Safe inside. Outside, I might be in danger. Nothing can change that. But the opposite could be true, too: I'm in danger here and safe outside. The calf isn't always so smart to hide in the slaughterhouse.

Marie-Michèle returned with a glowing smile.

"I'm so glad I called," she told me excitedly.

"I see."

"He was about to go to the wrong address. Now he's going to come and get me here."

I didn't dare ask Marie-Michèle whom she was talking about. You always have to pretend you know everything. Everyone's secrets. That's one of the rules of the game.

"That's nice of him to come and pick you up."

"The girls were stupid to run him off last night," Marie-Michèle said.

We sat in silence.

"He's an important photographer, you know. He works for *Vogue* magazine."

It was obvious that *Vogue* meant nothing to me.

"*Vogue* is just the world's most prestigious fashion magazine. I never miss an issue of *Vogue*. If you ask me," she said, smiling a little smile, "Pasqualine really missed an opportunity ... That's what I don't like about those girls: they don't respect anybody or anything. Miki's the only one with something between her ears. Miki's got class, but the rest of them are right off the street, believe me."

She paused. I waited.

"It's true," she conceded. "Pasqualine's pretty, but she's got nothing upstairs. She was stupid to let a chance like that go by. He wanted her first. She's their type ..."

"Whose type?"

"The *Vogue* type. Tall and thin, no breasts, but that's not enough to succeed in this business, you have to know how to make your move. Do you realize! A photographer from *Vogue!* You've got to be pretty dumb to act the way they did. I let it all happen, I watched them, I saw they were way off the mark ... You have to know how to handle it. Of course, Miki stayed on the sidelines the whole time. Miki could have had this guy any day of the week and I know it ... The other girls are just too stupid ... But

107

Miki's already taken, good thing for me, she has a man and I'm sure she wants to hold onto him, that's normal, because all the girls want to get their hands on a guy like that, starting with me ... Can you imagine? He's handsome, young, rich, powerful, he leaves Miki alone, three-quarters of the time he's not even here, it's manna from heaven, and Miki knows it. That's why she didn't even bat an eyelash at the *Vogue* guy last night, a good thing, too, like I said, because otherwise I wouldn't have stood a chance ..."

A car motor rattled out on the street. Marie-Michèle listened hard. Her body tense, happy, like a vibrating string. Today was her day.

"I think that's him. I'd better go out. We're going to have a drink at the Olofson and then get something to eat. I'm going to pay my share, you know. I might even take him out myself." She opened her wallet and showed me a bundle of green bills. "I'd better not go out too quickly. He's still a man, after all ... Can you imagine, *Vogue?* I'll tell you what I hate the most, especially about Choupette: they think everyone is like Frank and Papa. They're so far behind the times with their shriveled up old men. I just turned twenty, and you can be sure I'm not going to spend the rest of my life in this country ... I should really go now but I don't want him to know what's on my mind ... Nothing I said must ever leave this room. Why am I talking like this? I don't even know you. Well, I'd better go."

As she left, she turned and gave me a gentle smile. A second later, she was transformed into a blood-thirsty tigress of the urban jungle, ready for the fight to the finish. No quarter given. And everything would be decided in the first few seconds.

108

# The Skies Open!

From the slough of my eyelids
—M. S.-A.

The afternoon slides gently along the burning asphalt. People walk beneath my window and suspect nothing. Busy with their own business. Careworn or indifferent faces. Sudden bursts of laughter. A man in a hat (maybe a shark, though sharks prefer dark glasses) crosses to the sunny side of the street to shake hands with someone. I don't hear the street noise. No sound. A silent film.

I can clearly see my house from here. Just across the way. You can't miss it. The door flies open. Aunt Raymonde comes out with my mother behind her. They step onto the sidewalk. My mother looks worried. Aunt Raymonde is angry. Aunt Ninine stays in the doorway. My mother keeps glancing this way and that, as if she were expecting someone. Aunt Raymonde is chomping at the bit. Time goes faster when you want to hold it back. My mother goes back into the house and comes out again with a package wrapped in brown paper. Aunt Raymonde tells her something (she really looks mad now), and she turns back to the house again. A man in a hat (a shark?) stops to talk to Aunt Raymonde, who makes a big show of ignoring him. My mother finally comes out again and bursts into sobs, all the while keeping up a conversation with Aunt Raymonde. The man moves closer to my mother and Aunt Raymonde, who pushes him away as hard as she can. He stumbles, loses his balance, staggers onto the street, where a car almost hits him.

My mother screams horribly (I see her open mouth and wide eyes, but hear no sound), and Aunt Raymonde hides her face in her hands. The man picks up his hat and goes off, muttering under his breath. My mother is frozen to the spot. Aunt Raymonde goes striding down the sidewalk. A little girl runs past and motions to my mother, who lifts her head. Aunt Raymonde looks toward the sky, too. A man runs across the street. The skies open. Everyone panics. The street changes its face. A cyclist dashes across my field of vision. He wants to get home before the cloudburst. Drops are already hitting the windowpane. Then, suddenly, streams of water fall from the sky. The street is empty. Aunt Raymonde looks disoriented. My mother starts sobbing again. Aunt Raymonde tries to pull her into the house. It's a real downpour. I can hardly see what's happening on the other side of the street. The picture is blurry, like in the canvases by Beauvoir, the painter from Carrefour. The rain comes down twice as hard. I can't see a thing. All I can do is watch it fall. The sewers are overflowing. The street is worse than a river. I see a bed go by with a man lying on top of it. Cars are literally floating. A taxi driver struggles to keep his in the middle of the pavement. Suddenly, the rain halts, as quickly as it began. The sky is cloudless blue again. My mother is still standing there, by the wall. The bottom of her dress is muddy. Aunt Raymonde comes out of the house just as a Chevrolet pulls up next to my mother. Aunt Raymonde gets in next to the driver who's wearing dark glasses. My mother sits in back.

## SCENE XXI

# The Sunny Side of the Street

Godless livid fragile heart
—M. S.-A.

I'm already dead. Enclosed in a glass coffin. I see and understand everything, but I can't speak. I move my lips, but no one hears. I am on the other side of things. The shadow side. The light is just across the way. That's how I feel when I look at my room on the other side of the street. I see myself there, doing my homework, studying my lessons. I'm a good boy. Or so my mother and my aunts think. Meanwhile, I'm full of rage. Angry at everything. I hate this house, I hate this city. I want the sky all to myself. No one suspects what's really going on inside me. I display obedience. I obey my mother, I obey my aunts, I obey my teachers—though I hate them all. The only time I feel alive is when I think about the girls. Fortunately, they're always there. Just across the way, at Miki's house. That's the only good thing in life: the girls. Especially when you have time to think about them, the way I do. I've got plenty of time on my hands. The result of being a good boy. I always finish my homework and my lessons on time. I put away my notebooks and books in my desk and go lie down. I lie on my back and stare at the ceiling until it turns into a sky. Then I get up and go to the window. I look across the way, to Miki's. They're there, thank God. They're always there. They'll be there till the end of time. The divine covenant. Where do all these girls come from? They're everywhere. In the street, at school, at the market, in front of the Paramount, on the Place Saint-Alexandre, on the Champs-de-Mars, by the Portail Léogâne, at the Stadium (especially when Violette's playing). There are hundreds of them, but Pasqualine rules my dreams. I can watch her for hours from the window of my room until my head starts spinning. I devour her long, slender body. I burn her image into my mind, my arms, my belly, my legs, my hands, my mouth. Then I go back to the bed. I lie down next to her. When the image starts to fade, I return to the window and watch her again. Now I'm here, in the room where she dances away the hours. But to truly feel her presence, I have to imagine that I'm still across the way, watching her from my room. Will I ever touch her body? Her real body, and not just the picture I have in my mind? My bones hurt, as if I had spent the night in a torture chamber. I go back in time; maybe I really was murdered last night in the yard by the Macaya Bar. I clearly remember the shark calling out to me. Innocently, I went to him. I saw the woman next to him, making all kinds of signs. That's clear enough. It took me a while to decipher the prostitute's code. After that, I can't say exactly what happened. The answer is important, especially in my case. It's a matter of life and death—my own. How long does it take for a drunk shark to hit a man two meters away? How long did it take me to get the message the prostitute was trying to send me?

Everything depends on that.

SCENE XXII

# La Petite Mort

The gallop of the Antinea
—M. S.-A.

A taxi pulled into the yard and a girl stepped out. She walked around the car to the driver's window. Instead of paying, she stroked his cheek. The man laughed and backed his car out of the yard. The entire notion of money was being challenged.

She knocked at the door. I opened it. Half way.

"You're out of luck," I told her. "They've all gone to the beach."

She looked at me coolly, then slipped through the doorway.

"Who said I wanted to go to the beach?"

"Everybody else …"

Casually, she tossed her bag on the floor; she wasn't interested in my explanations.

"I just got the hell out of my place."

I've always dreamed of being able to make that declaration.

"Why?" I asked, after a minute.

She looked at me as if I were dumber than a cockroach. That wasn't the right question to ask. At times like this, you're better off talking about the weather.

"Do you know Miki?" she asked.

"I'm her neighbor. I live across the street."

With a girl like her, you couldn't make up just any old kind of story.

"I'm her cousin, Marie-Flore."

I'd seen her from my window. She must have been fourteen years old, and not a day more. From across the way, she looked older. I would have said sixteen.

"My mother's a slut."

Fighting words.

"Oh? Why's that?" I asked stupidly.

"Because she screws with that bastard."

"Who?"

She paused, but not for very long.

"My father."

"Oh, I see ..."

"The bastard did everything he could to screw me."

This time, the pause was longer.

"Ever since I've been eight years old, every man wants to screw me. Funny, isn't it?"

I didn't know if it was funny or not. I looked at her and waited.

"You're like all the rest. That's all they care about. Though God only knows why."

116

There was rage in her heart as she considered me. Rage and courage.

"Do you know why?"

"No, I don't."

"You don't know?"

She flew into blind fury.

"What are you talking about?" I stammered.

"You don't know why every man wants to screw me?"

Suddenly she began taking off her clothes. She ripped open her blouse. Her breasts emerged into the open air like drowned men coming to the surface. She took a step closer. I retreated toward the sofa. She put her breasts in front of my face, where I could lick them. It was like having two .38s pointed at me. All she had to do was pull the trigger.

"Go ahead, tell me!" her voice boiled with anger.

I tried to avert my eyes and escape.

"How do you like my breasts?"

I didn't answer the question.

"Say it! Say you want to suck them!"

I didn't say it.

"That's all you want, right?"

"Leave me out of this."

Finally, I took my chances and stole a look. It was worse than I thought. The breasts of a virgin.

"I want to know what makes all of you so damn crazy."

I had no answer to that painful question. Just a hard-on as stiff as a poker. She lifted her skirt, took my hand and put it between her legs.

"What's that?"

"Your vagina."

"No," she told me. "It's your mother."

Good God! Fourteen years old, and she knows that already. But she wasn't through yet.

"What does your mother say?"

"I don't know."

Definitely, I didn't know very much today.

"My vagina says, *corruption!*"

"What?"

"*Corruption! Corruption! Corruption and more corruption!*"

She pushed me backwards. I fell onto my back. Down into hell. She was the angel of death. I lost consciousness. The room turned into an enormous, living uterus. I was being sucked up by the great womb. The medusa, the mother, the mucous membranes. The sea, the secretions. The great vulva. The bottom of the ocean. I swam against the current to escape. Everything was pulling me back into the belly. Fighting the waters. I saw a feeble glow at the end of the tunnel of flesh and secretions. I heard the great waterfall. I used my shoulders to wriggle free. Head first. I heard the water. I opened my eyes. A green shoe was sitting in the middle of the room. No one will ever know all the power contained in a green shoe, alone, in the middle of a room.

# Bye-Bye, Poet!

Pain and poem outside of all cause
—M. S.-A.

Marie-Flore grabbed her shoe furiously.

"Couldn't you have told me it was here? I've been looking for it for ten minutes."

"I didn't know that."

"What are you doing?"

"Reading."

A surprise for her.

"Reading what?"

"Poems."

"Why?"

"No good reason."

"Did you write them?"

"No."

"Are you a poet, too?"

"No."

"You just read?"

"That's right."

As she spoke, she picked up all kinds of things lying around and put them in her bag. Most of them belong to Miki.

"Tell Miki that ... no, don't tell her anything."

"Okay."

She turned and gave me the evening's first smile. Mind you, you'd have to be starved to call that a smile.

"Bye-bye, poet!"

Almost an insult.

SCENE XXIV

# Ladies of the Evening

The sleeping face of the faceless sleeper
—M. S.-A.

Car headlights lit the room with a harsh flash. The taxi
drove on, then stopped a few meters further. Darkness
returned. I preferred shadow; it was safer that way. My
mother and Aunt Raymonde stepped out of the taxi. Two
weary shades. My mother, silent as always, followed by
Aunt Raymonde, disturbing the universe. They must have
been coming back from seeing someone who could pre-
sumably identify the humid cell in which I was currently
rotting away. Judging by their posture, the outcome had
not been positive. They must have been worried sick. I
wished I could call across to them and tell them I was here,
close by, on the other side of the street. Miki had advised
me to do no such thing. If I talked to my mother, the first
thing she'd do would be to go kneel down before some

121

shark, who'd listen to her kindly, promise her anything she asked for, then go out and crush me like a cockroach. My mother has no idea of what goes on in this city. She still thinks there are human beings out there. She's wrong; the city has become a jungle. Even Aunt Raymonde, who likes to give you the impression she knows what's what, has no more idea than my mother. I could feel my mother's sadness. I had to clench my teeth to keep from calling out to her. They went through the gate. My mother's best dress, white with a black collar. Aunt Raymonde stopped and pointed something out to her. The light on the gallery came on. From inside, Aunt Gilberte had seen them coming. Just before she went into the house, my mother turned, and our eyes met. I was in darkness. She, in light.

SCENE XXV

# Like a Plague of Locusts

My stained glass all in shards
—M. S.-A.

The two cars pulled up at almost the same time. I had just opened Saint-Aude's book. His lines penetrated my body. The girls stepped briskly from the cars. Choupette and Marie-Erna were still in their bathing suits. Pasqualine had wrapped a green skirt over her bikini. Miki threw her shoes onto the wet gallery. Papa said something to Frank, and Frank burst out laughing. Marie-Erna climbed onto the gallery and executed an obscene dance. Passers-by halted to watch the show. Miki mimed a dance with Pasqualine, cheek to cheek. A man who must have been seventy-five years old, and who'd been walking down the sidewalk on the other side of the street, crossed through the traffic (setting off a dozen honking horns) to feast his eyes on Marie-Erna's gyrating hips. The crowd was small

123

but appreciative. Joyfully, the girls stormed the house. The show was over for the outside world. For me, it was just beginning. I was the only spectator at this operetta. Frank had left his engine running. He wasn't counting on staying long. I didn't know what Papa had in mind.

They pushed and shoved to get to the bathroom.

"Since when do you care about washing, Marie-Erna?" asked Choupette aggressively.

Mind you, Choupette couldn't talk any other way.

"I started washing," Marie-Erna retorted, "long before you even came to Port-au-Prince."

"What's that supposed to mean?" Choupette demanded, as if she didn't know that Marie-Erna was mocking her peasant background.

"Would you cut the crap, Marie-Erna?" Miki said, trying to head off another quarrel.

"This doesn't concern you," Choupette told her. "I want her to explain what she means by that. Because my mother was never a whore at the King Solomon Star."

Marie-Erna leapt at Choupette and tried to grab her hair. Miki stepped in.

"Are you two crazy or what?"

"I won't have her mentioning my mother's name! That slut wouldn't even come up to my mother's ankle. If you had a mother, then you could talk."

Papa pared his fingernails. Frank cleaned his weapon. Everything was going according to plan. The fight moved from the hallway into the living-room. By now I knew the lines before they were spoken.

"How come you two are always fighting?" Marie-Michèle wanted to know. "Maybe you've got the same man or something."

I don't know how many times I'd heard that one.

"What would I do with a wreck like that?" Marie-Erna shot back, glancing in Papa's direction.

Frank went on cleaning his gun, which happened to be pointed at my stomach. Papa smiled sadly. That's not normal, the guy must have been cooking up something. Marie-Erna's barb caught Choupette by surprise.

"Everybody knows you smell like fish," Choupette answered back.

Marie-Erna roared, and Choupette screamed with terror. She'd caught Choupette by the hair. Maybe that's why Marie-Erna keeps her hair cut so short.

Papa and Frank didn't move a muscle. Papa was wearing that pale, immutable smile on his lips. Pasqualine finished brushing her long black hair in the living-room. Choupette began howling like a monkey.

"I'd have myself a man tonight," she said.

Pasqualine smiled.

"What about Papa?" Miki asked.

"I feel like some fresh meat."

Suddenly Choupette looked at me, as if she'd just discovered I was in the room. I looked away.

"What's he doing spying on us?"

"He's not spying," Miki said.

"He's nice," Pasqualine put in.

"You think I give a shit whether he's nice or not?"

Choupette jumped onto the sofa next to me, and Marie-Erna burst out laughing.

"I'm going to eat you alive," Choupette warned.

Marie-Erna was laughing herself silly, her face contorted.

Pasqualine put on a Tabou record: *Sou kad.* Choupette started unbuttoning my shirt. Papa took a handkerchief from his left rear pocket and wiped his forehead.

"You don't even have any hair on your chest. God, I haven't had one this young in years."

I backed up against the wall. Choupette advanced, her hips rolling.

"Are you afraid?" she breathed.

I brought my legs up to my chest. Back to the wall.

"He's so cute," Marie-Erna said.

"Don't even look at him. He's mine."

Choupette pulled on my feet. I gave her a swift kick with my left heel. She stared at me. At first she was too surprised to react, then she fell upon me like a tigress. Pasqualine cheered her on.

"Get out of here, all of you!" Choupette cried angrily.

I struggled to get free from Choupette's claws. She had me pinned. I hit her in the stomach, and she let go a second. Long enough to try to escape. But she blocked me with her right thigh and caught me with a resounding slap.

"Choupette," said Miki harshly, "that's enough."

She turned on Miki, hatred in her eye.

"I can't even have any fun around here any more."

She caught me again and climbed on top.

"Stop it, Choupette."

She gave me a liquid look, then let go of my wrists. She eased her way off me in slow motion, and just before she left the sofa, she brushed my cheek with her fingertips.

Papa hadn't moved a muscle the whole time.

126

## SCENE XXVI

# Has Anybody Seen My Yellow Scarf?

Despair biting its handkerchief
—M. S.-A.

Miki was wearing jeans and a very light, yellow-silk blouse.

"Has anybody seen my yellow scarf?" she asked.

"I've got it," Pasqualine volunteered.

"I need it, sweetheart."

"How about that? So do I."

The two girls modeled the yellow scarf for me.

"Who does it look best on?" Pasqualine asked.

A real dilemma.

"It looks very good on you, but I prefer it on Miki," I said.

The two girls burst out laughing. I'm crazy about Pasqualine, but Miki is putting the roof over my head.

"What a charmer that boy is," said Miki radiantly.

"A sly fox is more like it," Pasqualine added.

Pasqualine put on a record.

"Not Shupa Shupa again," Choupette wailed. "I hate those peasants."

"They're no good on stage," Pasqualine conceded, "but I like their record."

Choupette took up position in the middle of the room with an imaginary guitar.

"Their guitarist stinks. One of his shoulders is lower than the other, and his mouth ..."

Choupette twisted her mouth as if she were in excruciating pain. The guitar solo came in just as she was playing her pretend instrument. The girls laughed themselves silly. Suddenly, uncontrollable sobs shook Marie-Erna's body.

"Oh, shit," she said, "I pissed myself ... Miki, can you lend me some pants?"

"No, sweetheart. The iron is next to the wardrobe."

"What am I supposed to do with an iron? It won't get the smell out."

"I'm not your mother! Soak the spot and rub it hard. Shit, don't you know that much?"

"It'd be easier if you lent me a pair of pants."

"The answer is no. Take care of it yourself."

"If it were Pasqualine," Marie-Erna muttered.

"Can't you stop being so jealous?"

Choupette continued her imitation of each of the Shupa Shupa musicians.

"Do the singer," Pasqualine asked, getting down on her knees and pretending to beg.

128

Choupette did the Shupa Shupa singer with his endless sideburns.

"Stop, Choupette," said Marie-Erna, "you're going to kill me, I'm serious."

Pasqualine shrugged her shoulders.

"Still," she said with a little pout, "he's got a good voice."

"Who's talking about his voice?" Marie-Erna replied.

"Besides," Pasqualine continued, "when you listen to the record, you don't see him."

They listened to the Shupa Shupa singer's warm voice.

"I can see him even if he's not here, Pasqua. That's why I can't listen to his record," Miki said earnestly.

"You're all a bunch of snobs," Pasqualine accused them.

"How can you say that?" Miki replied with a laugh. "You're the one who hates the Gypsies guitarist."

"That's not the same. I can't stand men who dress badly."

"So what's the difference with your singer?" Choupette asked, snapping the clasp on Marie-Erna's bra.

"First of all, he's not my singer. I think he's got a nice voice, that's all."

"That's all?" Miki asked ironically.

"What about you, Miki? Who do you like?" Pasqualine asked coldly.

Miki was just about to answer when Choupette clamped her hand over her mouth. Marie-Erna wheeled around, as if something had just stung her. Choupette thrust out her breasts to imitate Marie-Michèle. She had her voice down perfectly.

"What can I do, Pasqua? The Beatles are the only ones who move me."

"Not like that," Pasqualine laughed. "You forgot the mouth. You have to do the mouth, too."

Choupette concentrated a few seconds, then did her best imitation of Marie-Michèle.

"You see," Marie-Erna stated, "I pissed myself again."

"Nerves," Miki concluded.

"Does anyone know where Marie-Michèle is?" Pasqualine asked.

"No," Choupette answered, "but I'll find out tonight."

"Are you going to see her?" Pasqualine probed.

"My network," Choupette boasted. "I can tell you everything you did last Saturday night, Pasqua. Four quick phone calls, and I'll know it all."

"Choupette knows who's fucking who in this town," Miki said.

"And where, and when and, especially, how," Choupette declared proudly.

"I never mind other people's business," Marie-Erna said with a look of disgust.

"Me neither," Choupette said haughtily. "But I don't like being told lies. I hate hypocrites. I hate people who try to make me look like the only slut in town, when half the country is fucking the other half ... You know it, too, Miki, everyone's doing it to everyone else. I just want to live. I'm not dead yet."

"Who would dare mention death on a Saturday night?" Pasqualine wondered, putting on her lipstick.

"I know all about them," Choupette stormed. "They've got their wives, but they all come crying to me."

Miki nodded in Papa's direction and motioned to Choupette to quiet down.

"Don't shush me up, Miki. They're all the same. They get down on their knees and beg you to suck them off, and afterwards they run all over town, saying how you're the biggest slut they know. But I know they'll come back. They always come back. My tongue is sweet. They disappear, but they always come back. Cubano'll come back. It's not my fault if I'm the sweetest."

She turned to me.

"If I wanted to, I could lick you to death. Oh, yes, I can kill a man with my tongue, just my tongue."

"Stop carrying on, Choupette, and let's go dancing," Miki told her.

"I could kill you and bring you back to life three minutes later. You don't have to wait three days with me. Ask Papa why he can't cut me loose."

"Stop bragging, Choupette," Miki said.

"Are we going dancing?" Pasqualine wondered.

"We have a choice," Marie-Erna announced. "Shleu Shleu is playing at the Cabane Créole, and Tabou is at the Ibo Lélé Hotel."

"Tabou," Pasqualine said.

"Shleu Shleu," Miki countered quickly.

"What do we do?" Marie-Erna lamented.

"A coin," Choupette told Papa.

Papa emerged slowly from his lethargy.

"Heads, it's Shleu Shleu," Choupette said.

The coin flew weightlessly, quickly reached its zenith,

131

then tumbled down, turning on itself like an Olympic diver. It ended its flight in Papa's wide-open palm.

"Tabou," Papa spoke, then returned to his usual position.

Pasqualine howled. Marie-Erna wiggled her butt. Choupette kissed Papa on the lips. She stuck her tongue in his mouth. Papa's right foot trembled as if he'd just put his finger in a socket.

SCENE XXVII

# Are We Going Out
# or Aren't We?

On the rail of melody
—M. S.-A.

In the end, Miki lent Marie-Erna a dress.

"I don't want you to mess it up for me."

"Unless some fool spills his drink on me."

"Miki is telling you to watch out who you dance with," Choupette advised her as she finished her make-up.

"What do you mean by that?" Marie-Erna demanded, turning on Miki.

"All those guys you're always rubbing up against," Choupette put in.

"Too bad, Choupette, that you can't get one for yourself."

"It's not my fault, dear, if I'm selective."

"If *that's* what you call selective ..."

133

"Everyone in town hasn't screwed me yet," Choupette said. "That's what I mean by selective."

"That's because they haven't gotten around to it yet," Marie-Erna retorted. "I've never seen you turn anybody down."

"There's one I can think of," Choupette said with a contemptuous smile.

"And who would that unfortunate man be?" Marie-Erna asked mockingly.

"Peddy."

A scream split the air. Marie-Erna leapt at Choupette like fury itself and grabbed her by the hair again.

"That's not true, you slut, tell me it's not true."

Miki and Pasqualine intervened.

"You're nuts, Marie-Erna. You fall into that trap every time," Pasqualine told her.

Miki steered Choupette into a corner by the sofa.

"You're going too far, Choupette."

"That bitch gets on my nerves."

"I'm not talking about her. I'm talking about Papa. Even if you don't love him, you know you're the only reason he's here."

"Mind your own business, Miki. I didn't tell him to stay. If he doesn't like it, he knows what he can do. I warned him. 'If you want to stay, stay,' I told him, 'but my ass is my property and nobody else's.' And he said it was okay."

"I know, Choupette, but he's still a human being."

"He's a bastard like all the others. If he stays, he must have his reasons. You'll see, as soon as he finds something better somewhere else, he won't even take the time to say

134

good-bye."

"You think I don't know that?" Miki murmured, closing her eyes briefly. "Just don't jerk his rope too hard."

"I don't give a shit, Miki. If they want my ass, they'll have to pay the price, and that's that."

Choupette turned away from Miki and cornered Marie-Erna by the record player.

"That Peddy of yours," she said, blocking Marie-Erna, "I'll pick him when I'm good and ready to."

The familiar scream was heard.

"I'm sick of this," Miki repeated. "If you break something I'm throwing all of you out of here."

"Are we going out or aren't we?" Pasqualine asked, irritated.

"Wait for me, will you?" said Marie-Erna. "That slut messed up my make-up."

"I'm going with Choupette," Miki declared. "I don't want to be with both of them in the same car."

"Let's go right now," Papa proposed.

"What's the hurry?" Choupette wondered, moving slowly out the door.

"If we stop and pick up Marie-Flore at Carrefour-Feuilles, we'll get there the same time the others do," Miki said.

"Unless Pasqua stops for a snack," Choupette added.

"I'm a little hungry, too," Miki said.

"We can always stop at the Chinaman's for something," Choupette suggested.

"Good idea," Papa agreed.

"I hate that bloated feeling," Miki countered.

"Why don't we stop and get a good loaf of bread at

135

the bakery by the Stadium?" Papa proposed.

"Then let's move it," said Choupette.

The Buick leaped forward, obeying Choupette's command.

SCENE XXVIII

# Men Are All the Same

Sleep now, my ruin
—M. S.-A.

I started breathing a little easier. Choupette left with Miki and Papa. Marie-Erna was redoing her make-up from scratch. Pasqualine paged through a photo-romance. I'm continually struck by Saint-Aude's lucidity. Amazing that a poet of his caliber is hanging out a few blocks away. I often see him wallowing in his piss at the corner of avenue Monseigneur Guilloux and the rue le Cameau, across from the cemetery. Saint-Aude, the most delicate, sensitive man in this crazy city. Saint-Aude, both a foreigner and the most indigenous poet there is. Saint-Aude is from nowhere. I know nobody who looks like him. When he wants to, he turns himself into an ancient Arab poet. In my mother's old wardrobe, a while ago, I found a book of poetry by a man named Hafiz. He must be Saint-Aude's brother.

Pasqualine put down her book and went and stood behind Marie-Erna.

"What's the matter with Choupette?" she asked her.

"She used to be my best friend."

"I know. What's happening to her?"

Marie-Erna stood pensively a moment.

"Is it a secret?" Pasqualine asked gently.

Marie-Erna began laughing.

"Please, don't go and cry again."

"No, that only happens when I'm happy. Right now, it hurts too much." She gave a wry smile. "I'm strange that way, I guess."

"Don't worry about it, everyone's strange … What's the secret?"

"There's no secret. She hates me, that's all."

"That's all?"

"I'm afraid so. I talked to two of her ex-friends, and they told me the same thing. You never know where you are with her. They say that as soon as she likes someone, she starts hating them."

"Why not Miki?"

"She's afraid of Miki. She can't afford to be on bad terms with her."

"What about me?" Pasqualine asked.

"With you, it's because of Frank. She never knows how he'll react. She's scared to death of the guy. Haven't you noticed how she never speaks to him, and how she always manages to be out of the room when he's there?"

Pasqualine placed her hand ever so lightly over her pink mouth.

"I hadn't noticed," she said with false innocence.

"Frank scares everybody except Miki. As long as you're there, there's no problem, but the guy looks like a real killer to me."

"He *is* a killer," Pasqualine said coolly.

Marie-Erna shrank back. I kept my ears open.

"How do you do it with him?"

"I tamed him."

"That's all?"

"That's all."

"How do you fuck with a killer?" Marie-Erna asked.

Pasqualine gave a brief, crystalline laugh.

"It's no different than with any other man, except that someone like him is more sensitive. It's like handling a bomb."

"So it's dangerous!"

"Oh, yes. But also very exciting. And besides ..."

Pasqualine laughed heartily, a happy peal of laughter. Marie-Erna stared at her in astonishment; I listened hard.

"And besides?" Marie-Erna urged her on.

"Besides, when he comes, he calls for his mama."

"No!"

"It's true. A regular baby!"

Pasqualine laughed. Marie-Erna laughed and cried at the same time. The usual convulsions. Pasqualine held her in her arms and calmed her. She stroked her forehead gently.

"I've never seen anyone like you."

"I can't help it," Marie-Erna said with a wry smile. "My nerves are all shot ... Listen, can you do me a favor?"

"What's that?"

"Can you lend me Frank?"

Pasqualine looked worried and surprised at the same time. Marie-Erna held her sides as her eyes sent out anxious appeals. Would it be laughter or tears? She tried to catch her breath.

"It's not what you think, Pasqua. I just want to piss off the Shupa Shupa guitarist."

"You're with him!"

Pasqualine opened her eyes wide. Her mouth formed a pretty little *O*. Her hands rested on her hips. Marie-Erna lowered her eyes like a child caught with her hand in the cookie jar.

"I know he's a fool," Marie-Erna admitted.

"They all are," Pasqualine said automatically.

"I just want to teach the bastard a lesson."

"How?"

"I'm supposed to meet him tonight. I want Frank to go instead."

"I don't really understand."

"He's supposed to wait for me, and I want him to think that Frank's my man, just for this evening."

"What's he got to do?"

"Nothing. I just want him to think that it's me, not you, that Frank's waiting for."

Pasqualine sat down heavily on the record cabinet.

"No, Marie-Erna. Frank might strangle the guy."

"I'm not asking for that much," Marie-Erna said with a half-smile. "If he could just scare him a little ..."

A moment passed. Pasqualine thought it over. Her forehead was wrinkled. A nervous tic pulled at the corner of her mouth. Suddenly, her face brightened.

"I've got it. Frank has a friend. The guy's completely

140

crazy. A killer, too. And he loves getting sucked off. Get it?"

Marie-Erna's face was positively radiant.

"That's exactly what that little bastard deserves. He'll never get over it!"

# Papa Ain't Dead

Desire howling its savage refrain
—M. S.-A

Marie-Flore came back with Papa. The others were already at the nightclub. Marie-Flore went directly into Miki's room. As always, Papa stayed behind in the living-room.

"You've got to have good eyes to read in the dark," Papa told me.

I turned on the lamp.

"It's better that way," he said with a little smile.

"When I read, I don't feel the time going by."

"You're lucky, kid. I don't care much for reading."

"To each his own," I said without lifting my head.

"What are you reading?"

"Poetry."

Papa burst laughing.

"I didn't know there was any left!"

"You mean people who still read it?"

"No," he answered softly. "Poetry. I didn't think people still wrote it any more."

Marie-Flore began raising a ruckus in the room next door.

"Papa, I need your help," she called out.

Papa gave me one last look, then disappeared into the room. I began to dream on a line by Saint-Aude:

Poet, lugubrious cat, with a cat's laughter.

I pictured myself, agile and silent. I turn off the light. I curl up in darkness. I await my prey. I have a cat's brain and fur, paws and muscles, claws and eyes. I *am* a cat.

Marie-Flore screamed. Sounds of a struggle. Another scream. Beating on the floor like a *nago* dance. Slaps. Papa's labored breathing. My vigilant cat's ears take it all in.

"Don't touch me, you dirty pig."

"Why don't you want me?"

"I can't stand your randy old goat's breath."

"Just a kiss, Marie-Flore."

"Go fuck yourself."

More fighting. Then silence. Papa was rising to the occasion. Papa ain't dead.

"What do you want from me?" Marie-Flore screamed. "You don't even have a hard-on!"

"We'll see about that."

"If you don't let me go, I'll scratch your eyes out."

The sound of running footsteps. Marie-Flore burst into the living room. Our eyes met.

"That bastard tried to rape me."

I heard the car pull away. Papa must have run out the back door.

"Shit," Marie-Flore shouted, "now how am I going to get there?"

"I don't understand. You would have gotten into the car with him after what just happened?"

"Why not?"

"But you said he tried to rape you."

"So what? I knew that old wreck couldn't do anything to me."

"Then why did you scream?"

"I wanted to excite him a little."

"I don't get it, Marie-Flore."

"I wanted to see how far he would go."

"And?"

"And the fool got scared off. I don't want him telling everybody what happened."

"It's hardly in his interest."

"Fools don't always recognize their interest. I don't want Choupette to think I'm trying to steal her bankroll. Anyway, what the hell, I don't even feel like going out any more!"

She sat down on the floor, back against the wall. I knew she wanted to be alone. She must be hurting somewhere. I know there's a war going on, and you're never supposed to admit that the enemy has scored a direct hit. But a wound's still a wound. She's only fourteen years old. To send such young soldiers to the front, the enemy must be in dire straits. The barricades are being manned by mere children. Barely women at all. They're the worst kind. No feelings. No desires. The head's the only thing

144

that works. Could we be in the dying days of the longest war in history, the battle of the sexes?

"Don't you ever go out?" she asked me suddenly.

"Sometimes."

"Where do you go?"

"The movies."

"That's it? You never go dancing?"

"Not very often."

"I go dancing all the time, and I never saw you. What else do you do?"

"I read."

"You already told me that."

How can a girl who's younger than I am still intimidate me? She watched me, both blasé and interested, from her corner. She doesn't know I'm a cat. A lugubrious cat. The poet's cat.

"You like girls?"

I was waiting for that one. Everyone asks me that question. Sometimes even my mother wants me to get interested in girls. But I reveal my secret to no one. I do not act; I observe. I've always been a spy. I want to know what makes this theater work. What makes us act the way we do? People never take the time to reflect; they're too busy acting. When you were my age, you must have been the same. I want to understand—not just some of it, everything. How does a man become Papa, for example. I have no idea. You have to wait, I guess, to find out. Wait and do nothing. Let the time pass. The river of time. I'm practically sure that Papa can't get a hard-on; Marie-Flore is right. Then what's he doing with all these girls? He's wild about Choupette, that much is obvious. But

145

Choupette couldn't care less about him. Papa is crazy about her. She toys with him. There's no end in sight, and no slowing down either. Somehow I get the feeling that it's not so simple. Papa's an old shark who's lost his teeth. They're the worst kind. He looks like a squealer to me. The kind that'll stab you in the back, then walk around and say excuse me. Why does he let himself be led around by the nose? What's in it for him? If Papa can't get a hard-on (if I believe Marie-Flore), what makes him tick? I don't have the answers, but it's not from lack of observation. I watch the ballet and see how the dancers move. The graceful curves of the girls. The massive bodies of the men. Why does the sight of a single breast make a man go crazy? Any man. I spend hours in my room working on that question. I can't stop my mind. Choupette can't stand Papa, but she's completely crazy about Cubano (the Skah Shah singer). Everybody knows he's all but married to the daughter of a big-time shark. Choupette goes hysterical if you speak the girl's name. Her name is Norma. She's fat and ugly (according to Choupette), but Cubano needs her father's protection. And that enrages Choupette. Papa will take anything from Choupette. Choupette will do anything for Cubano. I like Pasqualine a lot, but I'm more afraid of Frank. One look at his face and you know why. A real killer, a blood-thirsty shark. But he's Pasqualine's little lap-dog because of her black hair, her pink mouth and her little breasts. And that way she has of looking at you as if you weren't worthy even to wash her feet. Why does Frank worship her? What's inside that skinny body that can tame such a monster? Pasqualine's skin glows as if she were lit from within. You just automatically want to do

146

whatever she tells you to. Pasqualine accepts this gift as if it were her natural right. How did she discover that men owe her everything? Who taught her that? What's the origin of this cruel game? Why do we all play it? To seduce others and put them at our mercy. Some people don't even know the game exists, like my mother and my aunts (even Aunt Raymonde). Gégé, too. Gégé is a man of action. He likes to move. He hates reflection, whereas I can't stop thinking. I'm always trying to understand the world. I've always known it's all a game. I was ten years old when I understood. Aunt Ninine took me to see *Le Rebelle* for the first time (I've seen it five times in all). A couple was sitting in the row in front of me. They were kissing lovingly. The people in the theater watched them with indulgent smiles. Then I saw the woman slip a note into another man's hand, just as the show began. In that movie house, only three of us knew the real love story: the one between the woman and the other man who was smiling away the whole time. I discovered, completely by accident, that there's always a secret story hidden behind the official one. We never understand all that reality holds. A little detail will always escape us. If we hadn't seen that little detail— the note the woman slipped into the other man's hand— we wouldn't have known how the story really ended. That note meant, "I can kiss him all right, but you're the one I love. You're my man." With proof like that, all the kisses in the world mean nothing at all. Just a little saliva going from one mouth to the next. I was practically nauseous when I understood that. I was ten years old. It was as awful as a rape. Since then, I've kept my eyes on what goes on behind the scenes to see whether someone isn't slipping a note into someone else's hand. Gégé doesn't cry. He didn't cry when he saw *Le Rebelle*. Gégé didn't even suspect it was a game. A production. Gégé sits in the audience; I stand in the wings. I watch the actors preparing. I know their weaknesses. The costumes aren't always a perfect fit (this one has a torn sleeve; that one's missing a button). If you want to linger behind the scenes, the stage manager demands absolute silence. You must never judge or intervene in the plot. You couldn't ask that of Gégé.

The human mind is a wondrous thing. I weighed all those issues between the time Marie-Flore asked me the question ("You like girls?") and the time she came and stood in front of me. A little over twelve seconds.

"You didn't answer my question."

"What question?"

I played the fool.

"You like girls?"

I smiled.

"Do you like my breasts?" she asked, putting the same question a different way.

She opened her blouse an inch away from my face. I knew I shouldn't touch her with a barge pole. She put her firm breasts in front of my mouth. I averted my eyes.

"You don't seem to know what to do."

I said nothing. She was right. I didn't know what to do. I knew a lot about life, but not that.

She sat on top of me and put one breast (the smaller one) in my mouth. For the first time, I couldn't see what was going on behind the scenes.

# The Cry of Lunatic Birds

A heart preyed upon by shattered vigil

—M. S.-A.

## 1

I'm alone in the house now. It's warm. I hide Saint-Aude's book under my pillow. What are they up to now? I picture them tearing apart the discotheque. I go get myself a glass of water. Along the way: blouses, underthings, make-up lying on the floor. Miki's room looks like a coastal city after a hurricane. Mountains of dishes in the sink. Ashtrays full of cigarette butts all over the kitchen. When I think of how my mother and my aunts live ... Two diametrically opposed versions of life. I never imagined the extremes could be so far apart. Water. My throat is still dry. I lay down on the sofa, weary. The air is heavy with humidity. A storm is going to break any minute now. Automatically, I pick up Saint-Aude's poems again and fall asleep after reading this line:

A dead fortress where flowers of fear...

Harsh light. The camera of nightmare turning.
Gégé finally emerged from the Macaya Bar.
"Quick, let's go by the tracks."
I ran. Gégé ran. A Jeep was following us.
"What did you do, Gégé?"
"Don't worry about it."
"What did you do to that shark?"
He opened his hand and showed me a pair of testicles. His shirt was stained with blood.
"Why did you do that?"
"I'll tell you later."
No time for explanations. The Jeep drove into the intersection, blocking our escape. Gégé pulled me down a narrow passageway. We kept running. My stomach hurt. Breathing was difficult. "You have weak lungs," my mother always said. We jumped onto the roof of a blue house. Gégé pointed to a wall five meters high. He scaled it. I hesitated, powerless, facing the wall. The voices drew closer. I took a running leap into thin air, flying, my arms wide open. Gégé motioned me to land. I landed gently, breathing air deep into my lungs and stretching out my arms as far as they'd go. My chest thrust out, and my back arched. We started running again. Gégé knew the way. We came into a kind of clearing. The Jeep drove at us with its bright lights burning. I was blinded. Sharks came pouring

out from everywhere like cockroaches from under a sink. I froze in my tracks. Gégé tried to get away. They caught him and dragged him toward the Jeep with the help of their rifle butts. Gégé was bathed in blood.

"We'll take them in," their chief said.

"Where to?" a shark asked as he got into the Jeep.

"Fort Dimanche."

The name of that terrible prison chilled me.


## 2


The room was brilliantly lit. Sharks came and went. We waited with some other prisoners, all of us in handcuffs. All of them wore blood-stained shirts. I was the only one in a clean white shirt. Snails slowly climbed the walls of the waiting room. We heard the sound of waves. The sea wasn't far. You could smell the smell of crabs. Gégé was lying on the floor. One arm broken and a big wound to his head. A man was screaming uncontrollably.

"What am I doing here?" he muttered to himself when he wasn't shouting.

He stopped a shark.

"I told you I didn't have a gun. How could I have a gun, sir, when I'm afraid of firearms?"

"So where did it come from?" the shark answered.

"I told you. Somebody put it in the trunk of my car!"

"I suppose I did?" asked the shark with a carnivorous grin.

The man executed a curious mime: he put one hand over his mouth, opened his eyes wide and made meaningless signs with his crooked fingers. When it was all over, he retreated to the far end of the bench, his head hanging, as if his neck were broken.

Suddenly, we heard a strange sound, as if someone were tearing paper. Sheets and sheets of paper.

"The crabs are here!" shouted the prisoner at the end of the bench.

"What's that?" asked an old man sitting forlorn in a corner.

"The crabs!" the man bellowed.

"Crabs?" the old man repeated. "Maybe it's time to eat, but I don't care too much for crab."

Eternal laughter.

"They'll be doing the eating, not you," said a shark as he went past.

"What will they be eating?" the old man asked.

One question too many.

## 3

A shark came for Gégé and me and led us into a large, brightly lit room with an enormous black desk at one end.

A man was sitting behind the desk. Gégé was dripping blood, and I had to hold him up.

The man got to his feet. It was Frank.

"Give me that," he ordered.

Gégé walked slowly toward the desk, opened his hand and dropped the testicles into Frank's palm. Frank opened a drawer and took out a little bottle filled with white liquid. Carefully, he put the testicles into the bottle. Frank

152

considered the bottle a moment, then slipped it back into the drawer.

"You like testicles, do you?"

Gégé didn't answer. Frank stepped up to him and began hitting him in the head with his ring. Blood spurted out and described a perfect arc before falling onto my left shoe.

"Show me how much you like them," said Frank, pulling down his pants.

He pulled his gnarled, purplish penis out of his off-color undershorts. Frank moved toward Gégé and forced him to kneel, putting all his weight on his shoulders. He stuck his penis under Gégé's nose.

"Show me how much you like them, or I'll blow your brains out!"

He moved his penis dangerously close to Gégé's mouth, then pried Gégé's jaws apart with his hands and stuffed his sex inside. A second after Frank's scream, the explosion rang out.

In the convulsions of death, Gégé's body traveled half a meter as Frank fell to the floor. A few spasms later, Gégé died with a piece of Frank's penis in his mouth.


4


Almost simultaneously, the door flew open, and Papa came in with the girls (Miki, Marie-Flore, Marie-Erna, Pasqualine and Choupette—Marie-Michèle never comes here).

"Are you still working, love?" asked Pasqualine, kissing

153

Frank on the mouth.

"What's the matter, Frank?" Marie-Erna inquired. "You look a little pale."

"Nothing," Frank managed between clenched teeth.

"Are you sure, Frank? Are you sure nothing's the matter?" Pasqualine asked, stroking the nape of his neck.

"Can't you see he's working?" said Miki. "Leave him alone."

"Blood excites Pasqualine," Marie-Erna declared.

"We won't be able to leave until she's dipped her ass in blood," said Choupette, sitting down on Frank's desk.

Pasqualine stuck her tongue in Frank's ear. He jumped, then clenched his teeth.

"I'm working," Frank said.

"See, Pasqua," said Miki, "he said he's working."

"It's strange," Choupette noted, "the only place Pasqualine loves Frank is in the torture chamber."

Pasqualine shot a sidelong glance in Miki's direction as she went on stroking Frank with her graceful tongue. Frank could hardly stand up.

Suddenly, Pasqualine pulled off her blouse.

"Show time," Marie-Erna announced.

Pasqualine's small breasts demand an explanation from life. Frank is bent double. Marie-Flore spat on the floor, then moved toward Pasqualine, pulling off her clothes. Pasqualine turned to her, a diabolical glow in her eye. They came together, yet did not touch. Their backs bent in violent effort. Their breasts thrust forward. Pasqualine's serpentine tongue, Marie-Flore's wider one. They began to dance, and still they did not touch. Not far from where Gégé's body lay. Frank was on all fours on the

154

floor. No one paid him any attention. All that mattered was the dance: their arched backs, their bodies, their eyes. Everything is in the eyes. Pasqualine grazes Marie-Flore. The contact is made. The current leaps the barrier. Mutual shock. Frank whimpers softly. I try to make myself scarce in the corner. The one who sees but is not seen. My fondest dream: not to be seen. Pasqualine moves dangerously close to Marie-Flore. She brushes Marie-Flore with the tip of her nipples, but she's the one who gets the electrical shock. She grabs her belly. Marie-Flore dances toward her. Pasqualine lifts her head, looks Marie-Flore in the eye, then lowers her gaze. Marie-Flore smiles gently. The duel is over. So that's how women make love. Now I see why men, with their precipitation and bestial appetites, can't measure up. As Aunt Raymonde always says, "Only a diamond can cut diamond."

I made a move, and every head turned in my direction. I was bathed in sweat there on the sofa. Everyone was in the living-room. Frank and Papa were there, too. How long have they been back from the dance hall?

"Let's go to the beach," Marie-Erna said, yawning.

"What beach?"

"Mariani. I want to see the sunrise."

"I don't have my bathing suit with me," Choupette said.

"The place is empty this time of the day. You can swim without a suit."

"There's always that one guy on Sunday morning," Marie-Flore said.

"Sure. But he's the only one," Miki answered.

## SCENE XXXI

# The House Across the Way

The sound of my rising age
—M. S.-A.

I slept poorly last night. I remember the girls talking about going to the beach, but I don't recall much more. I don't even know when they left. Then I had that terrible nightmare. I was with Gégé at Fort Dimanche. I'd better get up. God, what a headache I have! I picked up a record from the floor and put it back where it went. My whole body hurt, as if someone had spent the night beating me. I drag myself to the window and see my mother in my room. She's just starting to clean it. The Sunday morning sun lights up part of it; the rest is in shadow. My mother is dressed as if she were going out. Her white dress with the black collar from yesterday. Which means she didn't sleep last night. The sky is already bright. Sunday's slow atmosphere. Deliberately, my mother picks up the things lying

156

around my room. Then she goes to sit on the bed or stand in the middle of the room, motionless. There, now she's moving. She goes toward the head of the bed, and I lose sight of her. From here, I can just see the little table I use as a desk (not the legs, of course), the wardrobe Da gave me when I left Petit-Goâve to go to school in Port-au-Prince, and a third of the bed. I can picture everything else in the rest of the room, though I can't actually see it. I can't see the little table or the pitcher of water that's always clean and cool (Aunt Renée looks after it) or the portrait of my father above the bed. My mother comes back into my field of vision. She stops again; she looks more lost than ever. I can feel her thinking about me. And I can't even tell her that I'm here, close by, in Miki's house. My powerlessness shocks me. Is that what death is like? My mother begins straightening up my tiny desk covered with schoolbooks, notebooks, bits of string, erasers. The desk is just storage for me. I do my homework lying on the floor, and I study in bed. Which makes my mother furious. When I go into my room, I throw everything I have in my pockets on the desk. Despite her displeasure, my mother never disturbs my pile. She respects my things. Aunt Raymonde is more efficient. When she cleans my room, it's very direct, she gathers up everything that's not put away and throws it in a big wicker basket. I spend the next week rummaging through it in search of my things: a ruler, a pair of underwear, my algebra homework. Aunt Gilberte laughs and asks me why I don't just empty out the basket completely; that would be easier. But no, I have to go fishing in the basket every time I need a shirt or a pair of socks. That's the way it is, that's how I am. I can't change my personality. My explanation always propels Aunt Gilberte into euphoria. She laughs so hard she has to hold her stomach. She slides slowly down the door frame (she never comes all the way into my room) until she reaches the sitting position on the floor, still laughing. Whenever we meet in the house, which isn't often because she's always in her room, reading, she never fails to inquire about my basket. "And how is the basket?" Then she begins laughing all over again. I picture her there, full of laughter, real laughter, healthy laughter. I've only seen her cry twice. Her door was half-open. She was lying on her stomach, her head under her pillow. I stopped and watched her. She turned around and saw me. She gazed at me a moment as if she didn't know who I was. Then her eyes lit up fleetingly and a vague smile touched her lips. "What about the basket?" And she started laughing between her sobs. For a moment, the sobs stopped and gave way to convulsive laughter. That was the second time, because the first time she didn't see me. She was in the same position, crying. I was so sad to see her that I went right up to my room without bothering to take off my shoes. When someone laughs so much, it's hard to see them cry. According to Aunt Raymonde, Aunt Gilberte will come to a bad end because she's too passionate. Men don't deserve such love. It's too much for them, and they end up feeling overwhelmed. My mother, on the other hand, is very gentle. The calm type. She never raises her voice, except when I forget to clean up my room for a longer time than usual. Then she calls me Sir and sets a date for a meeting upstairs, at the scene of the crime. I always have to wait for her an hour or two. She tells me about my father, who's in exile and who wouldn't have been proud of me today. At times like that, my mother speaks to me as if I were five years old (my age when my father left). In a low voice, almost whispering, she tells me how painful my father's absence is for her, and how much I look like him. I don't listen; I know it all by heart. She speaks at such length about my father that she completely forgets why we're there in the first place. Our conversation turns into an endless monologue about my father's generosity, how he always understood other people's problems, and everything he did to help his country. My mother stops crying then. It's worse without tears, as if something had broken inside her. Aunt Gilberte told me once (the only time she ever brought up the subject) that my father was the most amazing man she'd met. Pictures of him decorate the house. None of them include my mother. Most of them were taken by one of his friends who would often come to the house. In them, my father is always alone, and that has always intrigued me. He sits under a tree with his three-month beard or stands in the kitchen, his head all but touching the ceiling (my father was very tall); sometimes he is absorbed in a book. Never does he smile. I have a photo of him in my room. He's holding me with his arms out. He's just thrown me into the air, or he's about to, I don't remember. My eyes are filled with tears. The only photo of us together, and I had to cry. Aunt Raymonde is responsible for hanging up my father's picture on all the walls in the house. That's not the sort of thing my mother would do. I'm the only one she talks to about my father. She never displays her feelings in public or says anything. She's very secretive. Sometimes she says she has a toothache, and that way she can cry in peace. Aunt Raymonde says that if my father were here, things would be different. What would be different? Everything. She makes a grand gesture with her hand that takes in all of us and the rest of the city, for that matter. Yes, he would have cleaned up everything. In her opinion, all other men are hardly worthy of the name. Once she said that in this God-forsaken country, there are only zombies and sharks. All the real men are in the cemetery. Her lips draw back in disdain, and she spits on the ground, in the direction of the National Palace.

Once I overheard a conversation between my mother and Aunt Raymonde. I was playing under my aunt's window. She and my mother were talking in hushed tones. My mother was crying and insisting that my father had had other women, and Aunt Raymonde was trying to calm her down, but my mother wouldn't be calmed down. Aunt Raymonde began telling her to be quiet, and my mother went on saying that my father had had other women and had even had other children with those women. Aunt Raymonde begged my mother to be quiet.

"It's the truth, Raymonde."

"So what if it is?"

"You know it's true."

"I don't know these women, and I've never seen these children."

"But they're real."

"Not for me they aren't."

"But, Raymonde ..."

Aunt Ninine came into the room, and the discussion came to an abrupt end. Everyone is hiding something

160

from everyone else in this house. No one knows that I see and hear everything. They think I'm still a child, and that children are invisible.

On the way out of my room, my mother bent down and picked up something from the floor. Probably a dirty sock.

SCENE XXXII

# Day of Rest

Silence like a white crust of salt in a bowl
—M. S.-A.

I'm still reading Saint-Aude. It's a regular obsession. No wonder; it's the first time a human being has expressed what I feel with such precision. He goes beyond my feelings; he lets me read my future. Saint-Aude is expressing what I am and what I will be. He has a poem called "Sunday". In that poem are the two most terrifying lines in the literature of the Americas, including the United States. Compared to them, Neruda's poetry is awkward and decorative:

> I descend, undecided, without direc-
> tion, discreet, deadened, denuded, at
> the level of the poles ...

Who could have said it better? No one I know in

162

America. Not even Emily Dickinson. Dark Emily.

I have the house to myself. I prepare to spend the entire Sunday with Saint-Aude.

An hour later.

"Good riddance!" Choupette declared as she came into the living-room with the girls on her heels.

"I never thought we'd get rid of him," Marie-Flore told her in a voice that was a little too strident.

"I read an interview with Sagan the other day," Marie-Michèle began.

"Who's that?" Marie-Erna asked.

"A French novelist," answered Marie-Michèle, with her left eyebrow slightly raised.

"Stop it, Marie-Michèle," said Choupette. "You make us sick with that culture of yours."

"Let her talk," Miki said. "I want to know what she said."

"Who?" asked Marie-Flore, who hadn't been listening.

"Sagan."

"Satan!" Marie-Flore exclaimed.

"Tell us once and for all what she said!" Choupette bellowed.

"If you would just let me speak ..."

"Talk," Choupette ordered. "Express yourself, baby. Tell us every little thought you've got hidden up there in your head. We're here to listen to you. We're all here, and we'll always be here for poor Marie-Michèle."

Choupette got down on her knees. Everyone laughed.

"That way," Miki put in, "we'll never find out what Sagan said."

"Do you really think," Marie-Erna said, wiggling her

breasts, "that I want to know what Sagan thought about men? But, my dear Marie-Michèle, since I know it'll ruin your Sunday if you don't get your two cents in, go ahead, tell us."

Marie Michèle lifted her arms heavenward.

"What's going on here? You're making a big deal over nothing. I just thought of something Sagan said because we were talking about Frank and Papa ..."

"We don't want to know about men today," Choupette told her. "It's a day of rest. Get it, Marie-Michèle?"

"That's exactly what Sagan said about ..."

"Did Sagan get herself screwed six days out of seven, like all of us do?" Marie-Erna inquired, shaking her butt.

"Speak for yourself," Choupette shot back. "My ass belongs to me."

"Of course Sagan got screwed like everybody else," Miki assured them. "What do you think, Marie-Erna? We all get screwed. What would make Sagan any different?"

"You're nuts, Miki," said Marie-Erna. "I know that everybody fucks everybody else. You're talking to the wrong girl. Marie-Michèle's the only one who still thinks there's privileged members of the universe."

"I didn't say that. And I'm not going to say anything else, either," Marie-Michèle swore, then picked up her bag.

"Don't pull the same stunt you did yesterday," Choupette warned her.

"What stunt?"

"Your photographer," Marie-Erna reminded her with a mocking smile.

Choupette honed in on Marie-Michèle, moving every

164

part of her body that could possibly move, all the good parts.

"You should know, you little slut, that we've got spies everywhere. First, your two-bit photographer took you to the Olofson, then you were at the Chou Chou Train for some chicken, but you just ordered a salad because you didn't want to get your prissy little lips greasy. Next you were spotted at the pool of the Hotel Sans-Souci, and after that, you spent the evening at the Cabane Créole, and ..."

"Then what?" Marie-Michèle queried with a sly smile.

"Then, knowing you, nothing happened. You know how to up the ante, I have to give you that much."

"I do what I want," Marie-Michèle stated. "If people don't like it they can kiss my ass."

"No one's debating that, baby. But don't try to convince us that you're a lady and Marie-Erna's the only whore in this town."

"You're a good example yourself, Choupette," Marie-Erna said.

"What *did* Sagan say?"

There, I finally asked my question. I'd been waiting ten minutes for the answer. All at once, everyone turned and stared at me. By their stupefied expressions, I realized they had totally forgotten I was there. At last, my dream attained!

Marie-Michèle broke the silence.

"'Men,' Sagan said, 'are like soap. The more you rub away, the less there is left.'"

The audience burst into laughter.

"Absolutely true," said Choupette, slapping herself on

the left thigh.

"Did she talk about the white foam that ends up in your hands?" Marie-Erna asked.

"No, my dear," Choupette told her. "Sagan is anything but vulgar."

"How come you know Sagan?" Miki asked, surprised.

"Who doesn't know Sagan?" Choupette said grandly.

"Oh, the bitch is only bluffing," Marie-Erna insisted. "What do you think this is, Choupette, poker?"

"No. Because at least with poker you make money. Maybe you'd like to make a little wager? But all you've got to bet is your last pair of panties."

"The only thing you can lay down," Marie-Erna retorted, "is your bankroll, since what else is Papa good for?"

"At least I have something that's mine. Don't try betting Peddy, Marie-Erna, because you can't lose what you never had."

Screams. Howls of pain. The usual number.

"I'm going to make sure you won't lose your last pair of dirty panties, country girl. In case you didn't know," said Choupette, "Françoise Sagan is the author of *Bonjour, Tristesse, Aimez-vous Brahms?* and *Un certain sourire,* among other books. She wrote screenplays and works for the theater that turned out to be flops, and short stories, too."

There was a long moment of silence, during which everyone thought very loudly.

"As well as that," Choupette went on splendidly, "she drinks like a fish, loses a fortune on the roulette table, drives fast cars and has any man she wants, even though she's ugly, skinny and has a lisp ... There it is, baby. Sagan's got class. So, my little Marie-Erna, nothing to say? You came knocking on the wrong door, sister. Sagan's always been my idol. What, no bitchy remarks? Cat got your tongue?"

"Hey, Choupette," Miki said, "you've been holding out on us!"

Right then and there, Choupette burst out sobbing.

"What's the matter?" Marie-Erna asked, putting her arms around Choupette.

"What's the matter?" Miki echoed.

"My mother ... I was thinking about my mother. If she hadn't died ..."

"If she hadn't died," Miki said gently, "what would have happened?"

"You'd have been a doctor," Marie-Flore scoffed.

"Shut your face!" Marie-Erna shouted at her.

"Sure, Marie-Erna, you say a lot worse than that."

"You really can't shut it, can you?" Marie-Erna retorted. "It smells like piss in here, and it's spreading."

Marie-Flore was about to take a leap at Marie-Erna. Miki's sharp eye caught the preparation that precedes the attack. She motioned to Marie-Flore to sit still.

"We'll settle this later," Marie-Flore warned Marie-Erna, who was still consoling Choupette.

"I'm okay," said Choupette, freeing her neck. "I'm okay now ... it was nothing, really."

Marie-Michèle handed her a small embroidered handkerchief.

"Still, you do amaze me," Marie-Michèle said. "You know everything about Sagan."

"Culture is like jelly," Marie-Erna said pointedly to Marie-Michèle. "The less you have, the more you have to

167

spread it around."

"You must have been waiting to get that one in," Marie-Michèle said sadly.

"Now Pasqualine is crying, too," Marie-Flore announced.

Pasqualine was crying openly in the corner by the record cabinet.

"What's going on today?" Miki wondered.

Miki went to Pasqualine's side and stroked her hair gently. Fat tears rolled down her pink cheeks.

"What's the matter, Pasqua?" Marie-Michèle asked.

Miki turned and said, "Pasqualine didn't want to talk about it, but she's desperate. Her brother's in prison, and she doesn't know where."

"What about Frank?" Choupette asked.

"Frank can't help her."

"What did her brother do? I didn't even know she had a brother," Marie-Erna said.

"He forged the president's signature on some checks."

Spontaneously, Choupette made the sign of the cross.

"No one knows where he is?" Marie-Erna asked.

"No one's had word from him for three months. We don't even know if he's dead or alive."

Pasqualine began to sob violently. Her firm, slender body twitched like a fish out of water. She moaned through clenched teeth as Miki gently stroked her forehead.

"Her brother's not afraid of anybody, that's the problem. He could end up dead," Miki said somberly.

"He could really get killed?" Marie-Flore exclaimed.

The wailing and lamentation rose up again.

"You really have to shoot off your trap all the time,

don't you," said Marie-Erna. "Hasn't anybody taught you when to keep it shut?"

"I suppose you're going to teach me?" Marie-Flore challenged her.

Miki shot a hard, disapproving look at Marie-Erna and Marie-Flore.

"What can Frank do?" Marie-Michèle asked.

"Not much," Miki answered.

"Then what good is he?" Marie-Flore wondered.

"Pasqualine met Frank a few days after her brother got arrested. She was trying to see everybody she thought could help her, and that's how she came across Frank. He was the only one who didn't lie to her. He told her he couldn't do much for her brother. But she stuck with him because she hopes she'll get some word from her brother. It's top secret. Frank can't say where he is."

"But if he can't get him out ..." Marie Flore began.

"Only the president can authorize his release," Miki explained.

"If he can't free him, then why is she letting Frank screw her?" Marie-Flore shouted above the others.

"Frank can still protect him. He has contacts with the jailers and the torturers. He's in the business."

"What if he's lying?" Marie-Erna suggested.

"What do you mean by that?" asked Pasqualine, who was beginning to recover her senses.

"I knew a girl who was in the same situation you are. She had to sleep with the whole presidential guard, even though her father had died long before. And everybody knew it. If you ask me," Marie-Erna advised, "there's no sense trusting a man."

169

"She has no choice," Marie-Michèle said. "If you were in her shoes, you'd do the same thing."

"Hey, am I the only slut in this place?" asked Marie-Erna. "Choupette does it because her mother died. Pasqualine does it because her brother's in prison. When I fuck, I might as well tell you now, dears, it's because I want to ... I like to fuck, I like hollering for it. I like men who make me howl like a little bitch. When I fuck, it's the only real thing in this whole goddamned life."

"All right," Choupette told her, "you can cut the comedy, you're not the only one. You talk like you invented the penis."

I tried to act invisible. It was like attending some kind of perverse Mass. After all, it was Sunday.

## SCENE XXXIII

# Should We Send Out
# for Some Men?

The Chinaman weaves my death
—M. S.-A.

The intimacy of domestic routine. Miki pretended to dust off some records. Pasqualine stood by the Gauguin poster. Marie-Erna was sitting on the floor, reading a photo-romance.

"I like this girl a lot," Marie-Erna said.

"Who's that?" asked Pasqualine, who was aimlessly pacing the room.

"Claudia. She's in a lot of these."

"I like her, too," Pasqualine agreed. "I saw her in a movie once, a long time ago. She was with Franco Nero."

"Now, that's a real man," Miki said.

"That's strange," Choupette interjected. "Someone told me he was queer."

Marie-Erna laughed.

"Choupette thinks all men are queer."

"That's not true," Choupette protested, "but some guy told me that any man who looks macho is really queer."

"And the effeminate ones are the real sex-maniacs," Pasqualine added.

"What about Chuck Norris?" Marie-Erna asked.

"Of course," said Choupette.

"And Rock Hudson? You can't convince me he's queer," Pasqualine insisted.

"Rock Hudson? He's a regular fairy!" Choupette laughed.

"Come off it," Pasqualine begged.

"I think queers are the most intelligent and sensitive people there are," Miki stated.

"That's because they're almost women," Pasqualine said.

Laughter. Laughter mixed with tears in Marie-Erna's case.

Silence settled in. Marie-Erna flipped through her photo-romance.

"What about James Dean?" Marie-Michèle asked vaguely.

"Who's he?" Choupette wanted to know.

"I just knew it," Marie-Erna said, "that bitch was going to come up with someone nobody else knew."

"You don't know who James Dean is? That's not my fault."

"What are you doing here if you think we're all just shit!" Choupette burst out.

"I am the way I am," Marie-Michèle defended herself.

172

"I can't change just to please you."

"You can be sure James Dean never screwed me," Choupette said.

Laughter.

"You're talking nonsense, Choupette. Whenever you don't know what to say, you blurt out some obscenity," Marie-Michèle accused her.

"What's an obscenity?" Marie-Flore wanted to know.

"It's that slit between your legs," Choupette told her.

"If you're looking for trouble," Marie-Flore began.

"The hell with you two!" Miki burst out. "Can't you stop for five minutes? It's Sunday, even God takes a rest. Women can't spend five minutes together without starting to fuss and fight."

"Should we send out for some men?" Pasqualine asked with feigned sweetness.

"There must be something like that," Choupette said. "Like when you order out a meal."

"My dear, the system's been around for years," Marie-Erna told her.

"With free delivery, like at the Chinaman's?" Choupette asked skeptically.

"Of course," said Marie-Erna, "but it's not for you. What do you think the rich ladies up in Pétionville do when their husbands go on a trip?"

"Either that, or they go to the Macaya," Miki added.

The bar's name is salt in my open wounds. I wonder what's going on there now. I picture hundred of sharks pouring down the stairway, into the kitchen, along the hallways. Like cockroaches with dark glasses.

The girls go on talking, but my mind is elsewhere.

173

SCENE XXXIV

# Who Was that Girl with
# Cubano Last Night?

Dolores beneath my disquiet lashes
—M. S.-A.

An hour later on the same mournful Sunday. Miki is sitting on the record cabinet, applying nail polish. Her back is arched; her chin rests on her right knee. Her left foot hangs over the edge of the cabinet. Pasqualine is trying on a pale blue blouse. Marie-Erna examines her face in a tiny mirror she carries in her leather bag.

Pasqualine begins the hostilities.

"Who was that girl with Cubano last night?" she said.

Choupette was busy cleaning her ears with a cotton swab soaked in alcohol. The arrow hit its mark.

"Cubano looked mighty interested," Marie-Erna said casually. "First time I've seen him like that ... like a little wind-up puppy dog."

174

Choupette said nothing. Her eyes were fixed on some distant point. She went on cleaning her left ear.

"That girl was leading Cubano on," Pasqualine continued. "He was following her everywhere."

"With his tongue hanging out," Marie-Erna added.

"I've never seen him like that before," Pasqualine insisted.

The cotton swab was still in Choupette's left ear.

"You know everybody, Choupette. Who was that girl with Cubano last night?" Miki asked, earnest as usual.

"I don't know every whore Cubano hangs out with," Choupette shrugged. "There's a new one every Saturday night."

"True enough," Pasqualine agreed. "Last week, it was Gina. Poor Dada Jakaman. He's chasing Gina right into Cubano's arms."

"Dada's not the only loser," Marie-Erna added. "You know Nadja, who's engaged to Rico Mazarin, the singer for the Fantaisistes de Carrefour? Well, the other day, I saw her coming out of a motel with Cubano."

"Are you sure?" Pasqualine asked.

"Very sure," Marie-Erna said.

"Because Cubano never goes to motels. Usually, he borrows that little thatched-roof cottage Peddy has down by the sea, at Mariani."

Pasqualine hadn't realized how carefully the others were listening.

"You know a lot about Cubano," Marie-Erna stated.

"Of course," said Pasqualine. "I live two doors down from Gina."

"All the girls are crazy about Cubano, except the one

last night, by the looks of it."

"Last night, she didn't get up once from her table," Marie-Michèle said.

"And Cubano kept circling around her," Marie-Erna continued.

"I didn't know you were so hot for Cubano's ass!" Choupette shouted.

"You can believe me, dear," Marie-Erna replied, "it's not his ass I'm hot for."

"He's not my type at all," Pasqualine put in.

"They all say that at first," Marie-Michèle said.

"And you're one of them!" Marie-Erna cried.

"I don't care for the Cuban type. You know, with all those chains and bracelets and rings and gold teeth. A man's mind is what excites me. I like intelligent men," Marie-Michèle declared.

"Tell it to the judge!" Choupette raged. "You lived with Choubou for two years, and he's no bright light."

"Don't you believe that. Choubou is much more sensitive and intellectual than you think."

"Choubou, an intellectual? You disappoint me, Marie-Michèle! And here I went around telling everybody you'd read Sartre, when I didn't even know who he was."

"You'll see," Choupette predicted, still stuck on Cubano, "next week there'll be another girl with Cubano. He's always been that way."

"I don't know, Choupette," Pasqualine said. "That girl seemed to be running the show."

"Cubano has started down the path," Marie-Erna declared sententiously. "Who knows where he'll end up?"

"In any case," Choupette said, burning with repressed

rage, "that's the second time I've seen her with that red dress."

"So you know who she is," Pasqualine deduced.

"She was at the Lambi three weeks ago. That's where I saw her, her and her red dress."

"It's funny you don't know anything more about her," Marie-Erna said with a frown. "You're network's developing holes, my dear."

"There's nothing wrong with Choupette's network," Miki stated. "That girl just got here. She's from New York ... from Queens. She was part of Mama's gang."

"Big Mama," Marie-Erna said. "I heard that girl was the terror of New York. You know what she used to do? She'd go to a dance, go up to a table and slap a guy right in front of his wife."

"What guy?" Marie-Flore wanted to know.

"Any guy. She didn't have to know him. She's always got a real tough gang with her. Girls in the latest style, all of them beauties, none of them married. I knew one of them. They really know how to have fun."

"Jesus," whistled Pasqualine, suitably impressed, "so Cubano's got no chance."

"Not if you ask me," Miki said seriously. "Her name is Florence, though I hear they call her the Silent One. She never says a word, never opens her mouth, you know the type. She just sits back and watches the guy make a fool out of himself."

"Then what happens?" Marie-Erna asked, making a mental note of this new technique.

"Nothing. She keeps her silence, and the guy goes absolutely crazy," Miki concluded.

"That must not be easy," Marie-Erna remarked. "To be silent without looking stupid. I couldn't do it."

Choupette rose and went toward Miki's room, a dejected figure. Her muscles in knots, her neck tense and slightly bent. It looked as though she'd burst into sobs at any moment.

"She's really crazy about Cubano," Pasqualine decided.

"The problem," said Miki, "is that he knows."

"She can't do anything about it. When the guy's in the neighborhood, she can't sit still. It's a regular disease," Marie-Erna concluded.

"Too bad Choupette fell in love with a guy like Cubano. He's going to drive her out of her mind."

Marie-Erna wheeled around and turned on Marie-Michèle.

"The more I think about it," said Marie-Erna, "the more I think something happened between you and Cubano."

"Why should that worry you?" Marie-Michèle asked with a mysterious smile. "He's a man, and I'm a woman. And I've got everything I need. There's not a thing missing."

"What about you, Marie-Erna?" Miki said. "A little birdy tells me you wouldn't mind Cubano."

Marie-Erna went pale.

"I don't want to have any more problems with Choupette than I already have," she said. "I'm not a masochist."

"That's not a good reason," Miki laughed.

"Can't we do anything for Choupette?" Pasqualine wondered.

"What do you mean?" asked Marie-Michèle in surprise.

178

"We can't fuck him for her."

"I don't understand Choupette," Marie-Erna said. "She's always so level-headed ..."

"It's no different from your relation with Peddy," Miki reminded her.

"It's over between Peddy and me," she said in a broken voice.

"Since when?"

"Since yesterday."

"I don't get it," Marie-Michèle admitted. "How can something be over when it hasn't even started?"

"What do you mean by that?" Marie-Erna asked in a voice weak with despair.

Miki shot Marie-Michèle a hard look; Marie-Michèle got the message.

"Nothing," she said. "I was just thinking that life is strange."

"All kinds of things happened last night," Pasqualine laughed. "That girl and Cubano ... Marie-Erna and Peddy splitting up ... Saturday night fever! I like it when there's a lot of action."

"By the way," asked Marie-Michèle, "what happened when you left us, supposedly to get something at your house? You ran straight to the Cabane Créole and Peddy. What happened then?"

"That's no one's business but mine ... I'm going to go see how Choupette's doing," said Marie-Erna, her voice rough.

Silence fell.

"Welcome to the summit meeting of the Saturday night widows," Marie-Michèle told them.

179

"I didn't know you could be so hard," Miki said in a steely voice.

"Appearances deceive, Miki," Marie-Michèle said in a sing-song voice.

"I'll remember that."

"For once," said Pasqualine, "Marie-Erna and Choupette will agree on something."

"Men divide," Miki said pompously, "but misfortune unites."

"What's got into you?" Pasqualine asked.

"I don't know. It just seemed like something to say."

"Well, you're right about that," said Pasqualine dreamily.

An atmosphere of stylish sadness settled over the room.

### INTERIOR. BEDROOM.

"You slut!" Choupette shouted.

"Everybody's had a shot at you, Choupette! You're worse than a target in a shooting gallery!"

"You're finished, Marie-Erna. They won't even have you down at the Macaya Bar!"

"The word slut was invented for you!"

An endless, inhuman scream rang out.

### INTERIOR. LIVING ROOM.

Pasqualine's astonished face.

"Even misfortune doesn't last long around here," Miki said with a half-smile.

## SCENE XXXV

# Don't Move!

The final game
—M. S.-A.

"It's not that I'm hungry," Marie-Flore began.

"But you'd eat something," Miki finished.

"You said it."

"What should we eat?" Choupette asked.

"There's always brunch at the Olofson," Marie-Michèle suggested.

"We're staying in today," Miki decided.

"I want croissants from Chez Peters," Marie-Flore said.

"Good idea," Choupette agreed. "We'll all go."

"We'll take a taxi," Marie-Erna decreed.

"I don't have a cent," Marie-Michèle lamented.

"Don't make me laugh," Marie-Erna told her, "no one's planning on paying the fare."

"I don't like those schemes of yours."

"Well, then, you can stay and look after the house," Choupette told her.

"We'll be back," Miki assured her.

The girls pushed and shoved their way out the door. I decided to give Saint-Aude the rest of the day off.

"I'm not staying either," Marie-Michèle said.

"Are you seeing your photographer?"

"We're supposed to go to Kyona Beach. They're filming out there. Afterwards, we're going to have a picnic."

"Is he making a movie?"

"No, he's working on a documentary with an American filmmaker. He's the stills photographer. It's something about new Haitian music, you know, the bands, Shupa Shupa, Shleu Shleu, Tabou. They're filming a beach scene today. There'll be plenty of girls around, so I can't take any chances. You're never the only runner in the race. I don't throw myself at him, mind you, but I stay in the neighborhood. I watch. If I see there's no danger, you know, girls who are getting too excited, then I move in on him real slowly, I let him know I'm around, then I back off … That's how I operate."

"Does it work?"

"Sometimes."

"But it's not a sure thing."

"No. If the guy's the hurry-up type who likes aggressive girls like Choupette, then I don't stand a chance."

"What about him?"

"The photographer? He's cool. He's used to having girls around, he takes it in stride. I just hang back, like I told you."

"So it all has to do with rhythm?"

She looked at me for what seemed like forever, then nodded her head.

"That's exactly how it is. Rhythm is everything."

She took a step toward me. Calmly.

"You're not dumb, not dumb at all. I like your style."

"What kind of style is that?"

"You act like you're learning, but if you ask me, you know a lot of things already ... A lot more than people think. You play it close to the chest, don't you? Am I right?" she asked with an ambiguous smile.

"You're wrong; I don't know anything. I am learning."

"We'll see about that."

She stepped onto the sofa with her shoes on. I slid over toward the low table. She looked down upon me with her night eyes, then gracefully pulled off one shoe, then the other, and threw them against the far wall.

Calmly, she took off my shirt.

"Your skin is so smooth."

She leaned over and began to kiss me everywhere. Sharp little kisses. I laughed nervously. She stopped, considered me and smiled, then took my left breast in her mouth. I closed my eyes and felt her pulling me toward the middle of the sofa. On my back, my arms slightly spread, my eyes closed, I was at her mercy and hers alone. She pulled away from me, stood up, then I heard her light footsteps on the wood floor. She rummaged through the record cabinet and returned with Shleu Shleu's *Grille ta cigarette*. The room was bathed in the gentle shadow of Sunday morning. She didn't seem in a hurry at all, but my nerves were about to let go. She slipped my pants off. The

183

music disappeared for me. I felt my sex in her mouth. Something wonderful was going to happen. She stopped, right at the edge of the precipice. What exquisite pain! I bit my lip. This time, she took my sex roughly into her mouth. I sat up straight. She laid me down again and caressed my body. I felt her getting undressed. She took off her blouse and lay down on me. Her warm body. Her smooth skin. She stroked me with her breasts. My hard-on returned. Then she straightened to the sitting position and swallowed up my penis in her vagina. Slowly, she moved on top of me. I clenched my fists. She went on moving. I couldn't control myself. I was about to cry out. Suddenly, she sat roughly upon my thighs, impaling herself to the hilt. Time stood still. Then she began to scream. A rough cry that took root in her vagina and ran through her body, exploding through her mouth and out the top of her head. The body's voice. Her scream faded after endless seconds, and her body quivered. I was still hard inside her. Our breathing was in harmony. We didn't move. This was a moment of tenderness and pure joy. I was about to doze off when it started all over again. The slightest contraction and she began crying, making strange noises, pulling her hair, scratching her own chest, howling like a wounded beast. I hadn't done a thing or made a move. It all happened in her head. I still hadn't moved. She gasped for breath. What's the secret? Don't move. Love is immobile.

"Please, let me catch my breath," she gasped.

I hadn't done anything. I hadn't moved. I was too impressed by the mystery. She spoke to me in long streams of words, but I understood none of it. I didn't understand her language. She spoke to me with her eyes turned inward. I began to see that she was afraid of it. Her tongue was heavy in her mouth. She opened her eyes wide and stared at me sightlessly. She made desperate hand signals to me. What did she want? To stop. To stop doing what? I wasn't doing anything. I wasn't moving a muscle. The pleasure machine had gone completely wild. Maybe she wanted water. There, she's touching her lips with her fingertips. Water? No. She's choking. She grabbed herself by the neck as if she wanted to strangle herself. She opened her hands and stared at them as if she'd never seen them before. She clenched her teeth; she refused to cry out. She opened and closed her hands faster and faster. Her whole body was tense, stretched like a bow. Harder and harder, tighter and tighter. How far could she go? Suddenly, everything fell apart. Her cry was high-pitched and searing. The cry of the castrato. Interminable. Her body seemed to be breaking into pieces. She collapsed on my chest and fell asleep immediately. I waited, motionless and still hard.

Ten minutes later, she woke up and gazed upon me with silken eyes.

"I never came like that ... What did you do?"

"Nothing."

"Nothing?"

"Nothing."

She smiled.

"You're even better than I imagined. You're a real find, you know that? You teach me things about myself."

"But I didn't do anything."

"Shh!"

She put her finger over my mouth.

SCENE XXXVI

# On Sheets of Silk

Last lieder
—M. S.-A.

The girls returned in a storm of laughter.

"Did you see the look on the driver's face when Choupette kissed him?" Marie-Erna said.

"I thought," Pasqualine answered, "that his eyes would pop out of his head."

"Did you really kiss him?" Miki asked.

"I've got no prejudices," Choupette told her. "I kiss who I want, when I want, where I want. And if I don't want to kiss someone, all the tea in China won't make me change my mind."

"I'm that way, too," Marie-Erna insisted.

"Ha! You," Choupette said, "a good meal will change your mind."

"In a restaurant of my choice, of course," Marie-Erna

replied.

Everyone dissolved in laughter.

"I'm not a whore," Marie-Erna announced. "I won't take a man's money."

"Tell it to the Marines," Choupette scoffed.

"It's true," Marie-Erna said. "Remember that guy who had loads of cash and wanted to open a bank account for me?"

"Sure, but you were too dumb back then," Choupette told her. "You were just fourteen."

"Don't insult me," Marie-Flore laughed. "I'm only fourteen."

"And you're dumb, too," Choupette said.

"It's simple as pie," Marie-Erna stated. "I don't want money. I only want what money can buy. Get it?"

"Actually, I don't," Miki admitted.

"The guy's got to take me out to eat at a good restaurant, then afterwards we go swimming in the pool at the Sans Souci, then we go dancing at a fancy discotheque, and if he wants to screw me, it has to be on silk sheets. Get the picture, Miki?"

"You're expensive, girl," Choupette told her.

"If the guy wants to save money, he should take his wife out."

"It all sounds good," Miki admitted, "but you have to pay somewhere."

"On sheets of silk," Choupette giggled.

"I don't understand you," Marie-Erna said. "I'd expect it from a chick fresh out of diapers, like Marie-Flore. Sex doesn't interest those guys, Miki, and you know it, so don't try to fool me. They just want to show off. I

187

can't tell you how many times the guy's begged me to let him get a little sleep—on those silk sheets. They all want to be with a girl who has that tigress look. That way, it looks like they've got something between their legs. All I want is to live on a pedestal, like my mother used to say, every day of my life. He who lives like a rich man *is* a rich man—that's my motto."

"They're not all millionaires," Marie-Michèle pointed out.

"Of course they're not," Marie-Erna retorted. "But when one runs out of money, there's always another. There's no shortage of men who want to spend their money. Besides, I'm doing them a favor."

Marie-Erna began strutting around the room like a marquess, fanning herself with an imaginary fan.

"But in the end, there won't be anything left," Miki said seriously.

"What end?" Marie-Erna wanted to know.

"When you're not young any more."

"I'm not philosopher enough, Miki. Life'll take care of the rest."

"I used to think that way," said Miki, "but that was before I met Max."

"Of course," Marie-Erna agreed, "it's not the same thing. You hit the jackpot: a handsome guy, sexy, who probably knows how to fuck, who's rich and never even there. Everybody can't be lucky like you."

"If I were you, Miki," Choupette laughed, "I'd even consider being faithful."

"That's one luxury I can't afford," said Miki with a smile.

The girls burst out laughing.

"I was afraid you'd say the opposite," Choupette said, in the midst of a laughing fit. "That's my policy. I take it all: money, presents, fancy restaurants, hotel swimming pools, dresses, jewelry. I take it all, even things that don't belong to me. I don't give a shit about men. I plunder them, and that's it. I plunder the handsome ones, they're the easiest marks, the ugly ones drive a harder bargain, life hasn't been kind to them, but I plunder them in the end, too. I plunder the big ones and the little ones, the rich and the poor, the handicapped and the nice guys and the torturers. I ask only one thing of them, and that's to be a man. They can never hate me as much as I hate them. I am a plunderess!"

"Why do you hate them so much?" Marie-Michèle asked with fear in her voice.

"I suppose you love them?"

"I do. Well, maybe not ... I don't know."

"I hate them for everything they put my mother through. My mother was a saintly woman, and they took advantage of her for all the years she was on this earth. Try to understand, Marie-Michèle. I spent my childhood watching her wait for a man who never showed up. She gave them everything, everything she had. Now I'm going to get it all back, with interest. Down to the last penny. It'll be a thirty-year mortgage."

"All men aren't that way."

"You think I give a shit? They should have been paying attention, those bastards, they should have watched their step instead of crushing that poor woman like a snail. My mother was a saint. She never had an evil thought, let

189

alone did an evil deed. A real saint. Even when they stepped all over her face, she went on defending them, loving them, worshipping them. My mother worshipped men, they were her gods. They kicked her in the butt and she went on loving them. They don't know what love is. They're animals, and that's exactly the way I treat them."

"I didn't know you were such a romantic," Marie-Michèle said, her voice breaking.

"Go fuck yourself."

# Why Shouldn't I Ride Your Stallion, Pasqualine?

Final fires
—M. S.-A.

I hadn't had a moment to myself all day. And here I thought I'd be spending a quiet Sunday reading Saint-Aude. I didn't even have time to consider my own troubles, even though my balls were on the line, and that's no joke. The sharks must be looking for me, following the trail with expert precision. By now they must know everything we did since last Friday, from the time I left the house with Gégé. They must know we stopped by the Stadium and talked with the scalpers, that we went down towards the Portail afterwards, and stopped along the way at the Olympia Theater to see ten minutes of a Western. The ticket-taker must have told them that we looked like real killers, hot-headed desperados, the whole bit. Sylvana must have described how she refused to let me screw her because she sensed I wasn't a normal guy. The man in the dirty white suit must have told them that I tried to make him join a plot to kill the President. To put the icing on the cake, the skinny whore sitting by the shark must have explained how I kept provoking him as he sat quietly drinking a glass of milk (sharks never drink alcohol, everyone knows that) next to her. The whole thing was a plot. A plot with deep ramifications whose goal was nothing more or less than the assassination of the President. Which means I must have accomplices throughout the country, and abroad, too.

"Especially abroad," said the head of the sharks, with a glance towards Cuba. "If Castro wants war (a cold war, of course), well, then, we'll give it to him. In the meantime, whatever it takes, we have to find the individual who's put our country under a reign of terror since last Friday night."

For the last two days, my life has been traveling at the speed of sound.

Being wanted by every shark in the country is nothing compared to being a prisoner in a tiny room with six carnivorous girls. The one who's looking after me up above, my guardian angel, has certainly not taken the weekend off.

"Where's Marie-Michèle?" Miki asked as she came in carrying croissants, cheese, ham, sausages and cod cakes in a big wicker basket.

Choupette and Marie-Erna were carrying the drinks.

"Where's Marie-Michèle?" Miki asked me again, seeing that I was lost in my thoughts.

192

"She went to her place to change clothes," I stammered.

"That liar!" Choupette exclaimed. "I'm sure she went to that brunch with her photographer. It doesn't matter, we'll know everything that happened before she even leaves the table. Why does she have to lie all the time? It's like a disease with her."

"She can't accept reality: we have eyes everywhere," Marie-Erna replied casually.

"I'm hungry," Marie-Flore said.

"Why is she always hungry?" Pasqualine wondered.

"You must be blind," Marie-Erna told her. "Can't you see she's pregnant?"

"You're nuts!" Marie-Flore cried. "Who would I be pregnant by?"

"How about Frank?" Choupette probed.

"What are you getting at?" Pasqualine demanded.

Pasqualine doesn't need Frank, but he's her man— that's a local proverb.

"Look at her! She can't answer," Marie-Erna said gleefully.

"Dirty little bitch," Pasqualine hissed, with daggers in her eyes.

Pasqualine leapt at Marie-Flore and tried to grab her hair. The house specialty.

"Stop it, Pasqua," Miki told her. "You don't care that much about Frank anyway."

"I know," Pasqualine admitted. "But I don't like people going behind my back."

"Maybe he raped her, you never know," Miki offered.

"Men are bastards, we know that, there's no use going over that ground again," Marie-Erna said. "But the man

193

who could rape Marie-Flore hasn't been born yet. The opposite is more likely."

"Last night," Marie-Flore announced, trying to defend herself, "Papa tried to rape me, too."

Choupette wheeled around. Miki got in between her and Marie-Flore. These girls have an advanced sense of private property.

"As soon as there's a rape, Marie-Flore, we're sure to find you in the neighborhood," Marie-Erna teased.

"It's true, you can ask him about it," Marie-Flore said, pointing her finger in my direction.

Everyone turned to me.

"I was in the living-room, and it happened in the bedroom," I said.

"Didn't I scream?" Marie-Flore asked me.

"Yes," I said. "It's true. She screamed."

"Me, too," Choupette added. "I scream when Papa tries to stick it in me. But not for the same reason Marie-Flore does."

"Didn't I run out into the living-room?" Marie-Flore insisted.

"After a while," I said.

"After a while," Choupette repeated, shaking her head with a knowing look.

"And what did I say?"

"I don't know," I said, trying to slip out of trouble.

"Answer! What did I say?" Marie-Flore shouted.

"I forget."

"Goddamnit! Answer or I'll slap you!"

"You said you wanted to see how far he would go."

A scream rang out. It was Marie-Flore, barely saved

from Choupette's clutches.

"And what happened with Frank? You're going to tell all," Pasqualine threatened, "now that you've opened that big mouth of yours."

"Leave her alone," Miki appealed.

"No," said Marie-Erna. "The little slut has to tell all. What happened with Frank?"

"Did it happen here?" Miki asked.

"No," Marie-Flore answered. "It was at Marie-Erna's place."

"At my place!" Marie-Erna exclaimed, laughing and crying at the same time. "When was that?"

"Three months ago."

"Then what happened?" Pasqualine demanded.

"You were all at the Lambi Club. I went by to pick up a comb."

"What about Frank?" asked Marie-Erna. "What was he doing at my house?"

She started laughing and crying all over again.

"He wasn't there. I was waiting for you. He showed up. He was looking for Pasqualine."

"Then you jumped him?" Marie-Erna howled, clutching her sides.

"No," Marie-Flore answered calmly. "He came bursting into the house. He was looking for Pasqualine. He was absolutely furious. I told him Pasqualine wasn't there, that she'd gone out with the other girls. He beat his head against the wall. He kept moaning and sighing. When he got up to go, I offered him a glass of water."

"You slut! You know how to pick your spots," Marie-Erna said.

195

"I left him in the living-room," Marie-Flore went on, "and went into the bathroom. A little later I heard the door slam. I thought he was gone, but he was right behind me. He grabbed me by the waist just as I was about to turn around. I tried to get free. Then he started stroking my breasts. My breasts are very sensitive. I tried to hit him with my feet and my elbows, but he was holding me too firmly."

"It's true, he's so strong," Pasqualine said.

"He started stroking my thighs. I was fighting. He held me with one hand and with the other he tried to take off my panties."

"Did he succeed?" Marie-Erna asked softly.

Marie-Flore lowered her eyes.

"Then what happened?"

"He spread my legs as if I were a doll. I was afraid. I let him do what he wanted, but I pretended to keep struggling."

"My dear, I understand you completely," Choupette said ironically.

"The only intelligent thing you did since this story began," Marie-Erna told her.

"Can't you be serious for a minute?" Miki shouted.

"I figured since he was so excited, he'd come right away."

"Such experience coming from a child of fourteen," Choupette pointed out.

"Jesus! Maybe she could teach me a few things," Marie-Erna said. "I can't believe it happened in my own house. I'm never there at the right time."

"Then what happened?" Miki asked.

Marie-Flore concentrated for a moment or two.

"You're not going to make us salivate for nothing," Choupette informed her.

"The only reason we're listening to you," Marie-Erna told her cruelly, "is to get to this point."

Marie-Flore took a deep breath.

"All of a sudden he calmed down and started caressing me …"

"Caressing you?" Choupette echoed in astonishment, a smile on her lips.

"Caressing my clitoris," Marie-Flore said coldly.

"Oh! Oh! Oh Oh!" Marie-Erna moaned, doing a stationary dance.

"Go on," said Pasqualine, unshakable.

"He penetrated me gently, and I don't know why, but I started screaming and I couldn't stop. I thought he was going to come into me hard and that it would hurt."

"He caught you by surprise," Miki summed up.

Marie-Flore nodded.

"Did you come?" Pasqualine asked in the same serious voice.

"I couldn't stop coming. It's because he did it so slowly. I kept pushing him to go faster every time I came, but he never stepped up the rhythm, and that made me come even more."

"And he's so strong," Choupette said dreamily.

"How do *you* know?" Pasqualine demanded.

Choupette was speechless for a moment.

"Oh, shit! Why shouldn't I ride your stallion, too, Pasqualine?"

A moment of reflection. Everyone needed it.

Pasqualine's face was terrible. Motionless, pure frozen marble.

"You're right," she finally said. "There's no reason why you wouldn't screw him. I don't give a shit what he does."

"Well, hell, if that's the case," Marie-Erna piped up, "I rode him, too."

"Did you ride him, or did he ride you?" Miki asked slyly.

Marie-Erna made a show of thinking.

"I believe I rode him."

"I just wonder," Miki replied with the same sly smile, "because in my case, he's the one who did the riding."

Everyone started to laugh. Marie-Erna laughed and cried. It was going to rain. Marie-Michèle's picnic would be called off. There's nothing more romantic than a rainy Sunday.

SCENE XXXVIII

# Monday Morning

The exploits of the weary poet
—M. S.-A.

Miki woke me with a cup of steaming-hot coffee.

"What time is it?" I asked.

"Seven o'clock."

She was already dressed. All I saw were her nails and her mouth; both were brilliant red. The house was deserted. It had been cleaned, very early this morning, while I slept. Cleanliness and order reigned.

"You have to get up," Miki said amiably.

"Of course," I mumbled, not too happy about the idea of leaving the sofa for a swim in the shark pond.

"Max will be here soon."

"I understand," I told her.

"I'll tell him about your case."

I sat up and took the coffee. It was a shade bitter and

not dark enough; I drank it to be polite. She watched me. Miki is never in a hurry. I didn't feel as though I was being pushed out the door. She spotted Saint-Aude's book half-hidden under the pillow.

"Do you like that book?"

"It's strong stuff."

Not like her coffee, I thought to myself.

"Really? I never even opened it. Some guy left it here. He was crazy about Pasqualine, but it didn't work out. I never saw him again."

"You've never read Saint-Aude?"

"I don't have the time. Maybe some day. To be completely honest, I don't like reading much."

I recited a few lines. It's not easy to read poetry for someone else; it's such an intimate act. Miki listened to me and smiled. I realized how ridiculous I sounded.

"That's neat," she said.

Neat. She thinks Saint-Aude is neat. I suppose I deserved that one. But then again, maybe Saint-Aude wants people to think his poetry is neat.

"Go ahead, keep the book if you like it so much."

Too late to turn down her gift. He who reads Saint-Aude once will never be rid of him. I had no desire to become the reader of a single poet. I liked the way that sounds: I am the reader of a single poet.

"I'll be waiting outside," she told me.

Everything is over. She listened to the poem and thought it was neat, so she gave me the book. Some guy had left it behind. Who was he? She couldn't even remember his name. Miki lives in the present. I wish I could be like her. If I like a poem, I read it and reread it until I'm literally sick with it. Not Miki. For her, the past is what happened ten minutes ago. She's waiting for Max outside. She's going to tell him about my case and try to convince him to help. She can't promise anything but she'll try. I get dressed; no time for a shower. I can't let Max see me here. There's no time for niceties. My throat is tight. I have to leave, no matter what. By now, I know this room by heart, every centimeter of it. Every speck of dust. Every object. I know every article of underwear, too. If Max won't help me, I don't know what I'll do. Today could be my last day on this earth. I picture the sharks. They're swarming. They surround the house. They're after my hide. I touch myself to make sure I'm still intact. They'll get me in the end. It's a matter of time. The countdown begins. So soon! I hadn't noticed it starting. Here they come. I lie flat on my stomach. I crawl toward the window. Slowly, I get to my feet. Why am I panicking? I'm bathed in sweat. What's happening? I'd better calm down. I try but my hands shake. I steal a glance outside. Where are they hiding? Miki is standing on the sidewalk. She turns around and waves. Maybe she's trying to send me a danger signal. Maybe she's in league with them. That can't be true; otherwise, I'd already be in Fort Dimanche. I realize I'm panicking, and that knowledge calms me down. I try to keep my cool. A woman crosses my field of vision with a bucket of water on her head. She disappears down the long laneway towards Mademoiselle Anna's house. I want to be sure I'm not losing my mind. Am I seeing something that's not there? Alta's mother comes out of the shop with a platter of cookies. A dog barks loud enough to wake the dead. A second dog calls back. Is it night or day? I know the morning

201

sounds of the city. A handful of students go by on their way to Carrefour. They have to catch their *tap-tap* at the Portail Léogâne. Who's that guy coming down the street with his hands in his pockets and a notebook stuck under his right armpit? It's Gégé! What's he doing there? He's absolutely crazy! He's walking coolly down the street as if he weren't afraid of anyone, and meanwhile, every shark in the country is after him. There he is, strolling along the sidewalk, the way he does every school morning. He's waiting for me, he's got plenty of time. He can't go inside the house because Aunt Raymonde hates him. What's he up to? I don't understand. Either he really is fearless, or he's too stupid to be afraid. He leans against the wall, opens his notebook and pretends to study. His mouth moves as if he's reciting a lesson, but I'm sure he's looking at dirty postcards. I hear a car coming. I know the way all the cars sound that go down this street between six and seven-thirty in the morning, but I don't recognize this one. I hide in a more secure spot. The car slows and stops in front of the house. Gégé looks up. Miki doesn't stir. I'm frozen to the spot. When is Gégé finally going to start running? He goes on pretending to read. I begin to shake. I'm more afraid for Gégé. Finally, in slow motion, Miki moves toward the black car. Suddenly I understand everything. Miki is in league with Gégé. They're coming to pick me up. Gégé squealed on me, the traitor! What should I do? My legs are made of lead. But where would I run to anyway? They've got the house surrounded. The sharks are in the yard. I look more closely and see that Gégé's face is all bruised. Why didn't I notice that earlier? They must have picked him up last night and hit him hard enough to convince him to betray his friend. Miki steps into the car. She's talking with the guy at the wheel. When the car starts up again, Miki turns around and waves. A wave goodbye. Maybe she's signaling me to run. But my feet are so heavy, my head so empty. My life might end in another minute, but first I want to look Gégé in the eye. I want to see my Judas in the light of day. My mother just stepped out of the house. She spots Gégé. On my mother's heels, Aunt Raymonde screams and goes for Gégé's throat. He doesn't try to defend himself. Aunt Raymonde pushes him. He spreads his arms as if to say he's innocent. My mother and Aunt Raymonde go back into the house. Gégé is still there, leaning against the wall. I decide to do something stupid. I walk out into the street, leaving the door open behind me. I walk straight up to Gégé.

"What are you doing here?"

"What about you? Aren't you going to school? Your mother told me you haven't been home since Friday night."

"The sharks, Gégé."

"What sharks?"

"They're after us."

Suddenly, I go crazy. Gégé pins me by the arms.

"Stop it! What's the matter with you?"

"Gégé, don't you understand? They've been after us since you cut off that shark's balls at the Macaya last Friday!"

"What? You're nuts! That's just a little trick I like to play on people. I thought I'd played it on you already."

I stood there, incredulous. Gégé took out something from his pocket. For the first time I saw it in the light of day. A roughly hewn object made of mahogany. Two round testicles. Gégé stuck his finger in a slot and squeezed a little spring. Blood shot out and ran over his hands. Red ink he must have stolen from the principal's office; with his set of keys, he can get in there whenever he wants to. So that's what it was! Gégé wiped his hands on the grass. The ink isn't even permanent. Gégé gave me a shake.

"Go get ready. I'll wait for you here."

"Okay. What did you tell my mother?"

"That I hadn't seen you."

Just then, Aunt Raymonde came out of the house.

"Oh, there you are. So you've been painting the town, have you?"

My mother and my aunts poured out to greet me. My mother slapped me in the head as I walked past, and I stumbled.

"Don't hit him," Aunt Raymonde told her. "Whatever you do, don't hit him."

"Then what am I supposed to do?" my mother wailed.

"She's right," Aunt Gilberte said. "Don't hit him. He's back, that's all that matters."

"You know you almost killed your poor mother," Aunt Ninine told me. "You know you almost killed us all."

"It's all our fault," Aunt Renée declared, slapping her Bible with the palm of her hand. "I've always said it: we don't pray enough."

"What happened is completely normal," Aunt Gilberte decreed. "In fact, if it didn't happen, it wouldn't be normal."

"That's enough, Gilberte," Aunt Raymonde warned her.

"But what should we *do* about him?" my mother lamented, completely overwhelmed.

"Nothing. I told you, Marie. Nothing. We just have to grit our teeth and take it. He came back. That's all that matters."

"Glory to God," Aunt Renée shouted, brandishing her Bible, then using it to give me three holy blows to the head. "Let us give thanks to the Lord."

My mother and my aunts got down on their knees; I had no choice but to do the same. They began to pray.

"All glory to God!" Aunt Renée bellowed.

"All glory to the highest!"

"He's going to be late," Aunt Gilberte pointed out. She was the first to come back to earth.

"He won't have time to take a shower," my mother fretted.

"He doesn't have to take a shower," Aunt Gilberte laughed.

My mother shot her a withering look. In her book, the shower is a sacrament. I have quite a different opinion.

"Go get dressed," Aunt Ninine told me. She still looked half asleep.

I went up the stairs to my room. The process is called decompression. I started shaking from head to toe. My teeth chattered. I was still afraid, and I didn't know why. My nerves were shot. I threw everything on the floor. I was swimming in sweat. I wanted to wreak carnage. Even my father's picture wasn't spared. I tore up my undershirts. My mother has made me wear undershirts ever since I was a little boy because she claims I have lung problems. I pulled the medal from around my neck. I was in a rage. Nothing can resist my fury of destruction. They must have heard me downstairs, but they wouldn't dare come up. If they tried it, there was no telling what I might do. What's left? I picked up a pencil from the floor and broke it in two. A sharp report.

Gégé disappeared. He must have gotten tired of waiting. I looked out and saw him going down the street in that stiff way of his. Seen from above, he seemed frail all of a sudden. I watched him turn the corner.

A man came out of his house with a little radio under his arm. He whispered something into his neighbor's ear; she crossed herself and hurried inside. My mother's footsteps came rushing down the stairway. I heard whispers, stifled shouts. The news was official now: François Duvalier is dead.

"All glory to God," Aunt Renée said.

## SCENE XXXIX

# Just Crossing the Street Can Change Your Life

I'm here for five
—M. S.-A.

I'm leaning against my bedroom window, looking across to Miki's house. I picture myself there, a shadow behind Miki's window. I was there, scarcely an hour ago. I'm here now. I was here, three days ago, before I met up with Gégé in hell, last Friday. And now, again, I'm here, and it's Monday. In between, I was on the other side. Just across the way. A world away.